Dharmic Nation

Jagannathan, in his remarkable book *Dharmic Nation*, reminds us that the ancient and complex spirituality that props up from behind what is today called Hinduism, is a vast, intricate and many-sided philosophical system. One of its greatest assets is that it leaves to every human being his or her free will. As Jagannathan rightly writes: 'There is no straitjacket in Hinduism.' Throughout the ages, dharma has allowed all kinds of sects, beliefs and branches to develop freely. Even atheism is considered acceptable and a way to reach God (*neti-neti*, meaning 'neither this, nor that'). At every step in one's own life, the choice is left to the devotee to go right, left, straight, etc...

Compare this to other beliefs, such as Christianity or Islam, where on the one hand you are told you will go to hell if you do not follow its tenets and dogmas, and on the other, they imposed, often by extremely violent coercion, their religions on many wonderful civilizations that disappeared forever.

What is a dharmic nation? It's one that firstly follows, as much as possible, its own law of dharma—goodness, compassion, etc.—without however being weak, in a Buddhist or Gandhian manner; and on the other, leaves to its citizens the freedom of worship, that is so lacking in many parts of the world. I hope you will enjoy reading this book.

—**François Gautier**

(Gautier writes regularly for magazines and newspapers such as *Le Journal de Genève*, *Le Figaro*, *Le Point*, *Marianne* and *Le Nouvel Observateur*. He has interviewed eight Indian Prime Ministers, written 29 books, both in English and French, from *The Wonder that Is India* [1993] to *An Entirely New History of India* [2021])

This book is an important plea for Indians to support establishing dharma as the core political tenet in India.

—**Rajiv Malhotra**, author of *Artificial Intelligence and the Future of Power* and *Snakes in the Ganga*, and an intellectual Kshatriya

India is among the last two great surviving millennia-old civilizations, with the rest destroyed by invasions or otherwise. What made India withstand centuries of brutal occupation by outside forces was its innate dharmic way of life based on individual freedom and no dogma. The quest for truth is the idea of Bharat, ever evolving, ever lasting. In this book, Jagannathan, or Jaggi, explores what makes India, that is Bharat, so unique and what we need to do to preserve and sustain it.

—**T.V. Mohandas Pai**, Chairman, Aarin Capital Partners

This is a thought-provoking—and provocative—book. The edifice of any society is dharma and Indian society, and the Bharatiya nation, cannot be delinked from their dharmic roots. The secular implant, reflected in the implanted Constitution, was divorced from that history and it is right that these should be questioned, as this string of essays does, and not be accepted as axiomatic.

—**Bibek Debroy**, scholar-translator of the Ramayana and Mahabharata, and Chairman, Economic Advisory Committee to the Prime Minister of India

At last a thoughtful book about India's civilizational nationhood that takes on both colonial and neocolonial narratives that have dominated the conversation for two long centuries. Jagannathan takes apart each issue and presents a fresh look at a topic that animates intellectual, political and everyday discussions about India. Rarely is such a heated topic presented in such a cool and sane manner.

—**Sanjeev Sanyal**, economist and writer

Dharmic Nation

FREEING BHARAT, REMAKING INDIA

R. Jagannathan

RUPA

First published by
Rupa Publications India Pvt. Ltd 2023
7/16, Ansari Road, Daryaganj
New Delhi 110002

Sales Centres:

Allahabad Bengaluru Chennai
Hyderabad Jaipur Kathmandu
Kolkata Mumbai

P-ISBN: 978-93-5520-977-1
E-ISBN: 978-93-5520-978-8

First impression 2023

10 9 8 7 6 5 4 3 2 1

Printed in India

CONTENTS

INTRODUCTION

The Freeing of Bharat, and the Rediscovery of Dharma

Despite the title, this book is not about dharma, except in a general, explorative sense. I claim no special insights into the word. There are far better experts to tell you what dharma is, or what it means in today's context, but I am willing to try to get back on that path of learning. Nor is the book about Hinduism, Jainism, Buddhism and Sikhism, on which subjects, too, there are better experts to consult. However, these religions can be considered the four major pillars that grew and built strong foundations to co-create a composite civilization on this soil based on the idea of dharma, and around whom the rest of Bharat's traditions stand or have grown, each supporting the other through invisible linkages.

However, in an indirect way, this book does talk about dharma and Hinduism, inter alia, for a reason. The fuzzy idea of dharma, which means 'that which upholds', right conduct, personal responsibility, integrity and ethical behaviour—or a mix of these—in these four pillar religions, is critical to the ideas that germinated in India that is Bharat. It is not a western import, and it is not all about religion. It transcends the idea of religion as defined in the Judaic, Christian and Islamic—i.e. Abrahamic—context and contributes to our idea of nationhood. The idea of dharma broadly represents continuity with change, with the emphasis shifting in various eras. Sanatan dharma stands for something 'eternal', which, however, implies a willingness to change with the times without sacrificing the core values that must remain fairly stable. It is not about being static and mired in one idea. Sanatan dharma, to me, thus means 'never changing *and* ever changing'.

The book is a call to *all* Indians to return to the challenges of rediscovering the path to dharma, and this call includes followers of Islam and Christianity, the two non-dharmic creeds in our midst. It is also an exhortation to all dharmic peoples, not only in India but all over the world, to unshackle themselves from the burdens of colonial ideas, which made us a self-loathing people.

Colonialism, apart from the physical, social and economic indignities it heaped on the conquered, did more harm by capturing the minds of the colonized. Thanks to two different colonizations of Bharat over the last 1,000 and odd years, one being Islam and the other British (including their Christian faith), we have internalized all their critiques about us. We—essentially the elite—have grown to believe that Hinduism is mostly backward and possibly evil, that we are fools to worship 'idols', or even monkeys, snakes and trees, that we are nothing but caste, caste, caste, which again is purely a system of oppression, that western ideals represent the new, inclusive universalism that all modern peoples must embrace (liberty, equality and fraternity), and even that India is neither a country nor a civilization. It is just a collection of odds and ends in terms of religious and other things that define a people as one.

This is balderdash. Leaving aside the mistake we made in failing to reform the *varna-jati*[1] construct quickly, we have very little to be ashamed of. On the contrary, if we employ a bit of *purva paksha,* i.e. reverse our gaze to the notions we have blindly accepted as key to our current ideas about nationhood, we will find that it is the Abrahamic ideals that need re-examining. Everything they accused us of is present in them in multiples thereof.

They talk of free will, when their idea of it is the imprisonment of free enquiry on issues they considered closed—especially in matters of faith. Between them, early Christianity and Islam closed the Abrahamic mind. You don't have to take my word for it. You could read Charles Freeman's *The Closing of the Western Mind: The Rise of Faith and the Fall of Reason*, or Robert R. Reilly's *The Closing of the Muslim Mind: How Intellectual Suicide Created the Modern Islamist Crisis.* Christianity, despite claiming to be the worthy successor of Hellenism and the pagan world that went before it, destroyed everything that was great and noble in their inheritance. Islam did worse, by destroying Christianity and Judaism in the old world. They talk of free speech, but free speech without the exercise of personal restraint ultimately results in abuse and debasement of dialogue and argumentation. But in their way of thinking, the last free-thinking exercise between God and man happened either 2,000 or 1,400 years ago. Contrast that with the dharmic experience, where the spiritual conversation between man and God, or man and his higher self, is continuous, and exalted and enlightened individuals can repeatedly connect with God or higher truths without restrictions.

In fact, our gods themselves encourage you to exercise

your judgement after they have delivered their secret knowledge.

In the Bhagavad Gita, Shri Krishna, after revealing himself and the eternal truths to his disciple Arjuna, tells him to make his own judgement call. In Chapter 18, Verse 63, he says:

> इति ते ज्ञानमाख्यातं गुह्याद्गुह्यतरं मया ।
> विमृश्यैतदशषेण यथेच्छसि तथा कुरु ॥63॥
>
> *iti te jñānam ākhyātaṁ guhyād guhyataraṁ mayā*
> *vimṛiśhyaitad aśheṣheṇa yathechchhasi tathā kuru*
>
> (I have thus explained to you this knowledge that is more secret than all secrets. Ponder over it deeply, and then do as you wish.)

And yet, despite Shri Krishna telling Arjuna that the knowledge he revealed is 'more secret than all secrets', Sanjaya, who is eavesdropping on the conversation and regurgitates it all to his blind king Dhritarashtra, exclaims (Chapter 18, Verse 74):

> सञ्जय उवाच ।
> इत्यहं वासुदेवस्य पार्थस्य च महात्मनः ।
> संवादमिममश्रौषमद्भुतं रोमहर्षणम् ॥74॥
>
> *Sañjaya uvācha*
> *ity ahaṁ vāsudevasya pārthasya cha mahātmanaḥ*
> *saṁvādam imam aśhrauṣham adbhutaṁ roma-harṣhaṇam*
>
> (Sanjaya said: 'Thus have I heard the conversation of two great mahatmas, Vasudeva [i.e. Shri Krishna] and Partha [i.e. Arjuna]. And so wonderful is that message that my hair is standing on end.') (Loose translation)

And nor is this something that occurs only in the Gita. In Goswami Tulsidas's Ramayana, *Shri Ram Charit Manas*, written in the sixteenth century, which was centuries after the Gita was composed, Shri Rama does the same thing—even after delivering a divine discourse to his people, he says the choice is yours.

Verses 34 and 35 in *Shri Ram Charit Manas* run thus:

Eka bāra raghunātha bolāe, guru dwija purabāsī saba āe
nahiṅ anīti nahiṅ kachhu prabhutāī, sunahu karahu jo tumhahi sohāī

The Lord, Raghunatha (i.e. Shri Rama), apparently called his people and even his Guru (Vashishta) to speak to them about the truths he knew, but in the end, he humbly said: 'The advice I have given to you is neither untrue nor a God's decree. Pay attention, mull over it, and then do what you wish.' (Rough translation)

Consider the humility Tulsidas invested in the character of Shri Rama, where a God tells his people that he has not told them anything incorrect, and that there is no divine coercion to accept it. They have to understand what he said and do what they think fit. Is this free will, free choice, or the exhortations of Abrahamic gods, who tell their followers, 'Worship me, or else... My way or the highway'?

The West talks of freedom of religion, but their idea of that is the same as Henry Ford's dictum about the choice of colour for his Model T automobile: any colour, so long as it is black. In Abrahamic theology, you can choose any God so long as it is *their* God. And the three Abrahamic religions—Judaism, Christianity and Islam—that share this idea cannot even agree on which God, even though they largely agree on the genealogy of their historical prophets and gods.

Just because God and religion have been defined in a specific way by the Abrahamic world, it cannot be imposed on others. That would be intellectual colonialism of the worst kind. If, in the Abrahamic context, Hinduism is not a religion, it should be equally possible for Hindus to redefine the Abrahamic religions as non-religions.[2]

In fact, Abrahamic religions are more about politics than religiosity or spirituality. Nobody would object to a Muslim praying five times a day, but surely one can object to him occupying public spaces for the same? The first part is religion, the second part is a kind of imposition on others, and hence about asserting political muscle.

Nothing I am saying here has not been said by brighter Hindu philosophers (or even atheists in the western tradition) a long time before me, but it needs reiteration because the Abrahamics cannot presume—and get away with—the idea that only their definitions are valid. They are not, and often they don't make sense.

Religion should be about empowering individuals to seek paths to God, to sacred spaces, to higher ways of experiencing the truth and the larger realities of the cosmos, and it is in these aspects that the fundamental differences between Abrahamic and dharmic traditions lie.

Abrahamic systems are about *belief*, about arbitrarily deciding who is God and stopping further explorations of the idea of God and sacred spaces. The empowerment in dharmic traditions comes from the fact that dharma is not about giving each individual the same goal, never mind his capabilities, but a chance to find out what is his *svadharma*, his individual nature, and allowing him to decide how he can serve dharma. The individual makes his choices according to his life situation. Also, the karmic system talks about rebirth, which implies that an individual gets more chances to make good. In the Abrahamic system, there is one life, and if you have failed God, you go to hell. Failure is not an option.

Dharmic approaches, on the other hand, privilege high-quality doubt and knowledge-seeking over blind or incontrovertible faith; they are a journey of discovery rather than of an arrival at a destination. Choosing a likely path to God means that one need not arrive at a final conclusion based on emphatic assertions in unprovable holy texts. A path, if not fruitful in terms of experience and insight, can be abandoned and another chosen.

In short, Abrahamic faiths are about excluding free enquiry into the idea of God. Indic faiths are open-ended and capable of course-correction.

Worse, at least in my view, the Abrahamic idea is about putting God in a straitjacket, converting Him/Her/It into a bigot and debasing them in the process. I deliberately use the word 'It' as an additional option for describing God, for the real God or Ultimate Truth—assuming humans can ever get to that stage—may be neither male nor female, nor even someone imaginable in human, animal or arboreal form. The Abrahamic God is what He says He is, and humans have to live with the definition given by someone whose existence cannot be proved. How reductive is that idea as opposed to the dharmic one of exploring higher truths?

In the early Mosaic tradition, God was first converted into a bigot, where He refuses to share space with other gods. While we find jealous gods even in Hindu stories and traditions, there is no real requirement to elevate this into eternal hatred for followers of other gods. There is nothing structural in Hinduism that converts gods into implacable hate-mongers with no tolerance for 'the other'. The Abrahamics converted God into someone who can't stand non-believers or believers in rival gods. God is thus an insecure entity, not even confident about His/Her/Its own reality.

As the late Ram Swarup, one of the first Hindus to do a purva paksha on Abrahamic religions, said in his book, *Hindu View of Christianity and Islam*, 'Here everything takes place through a proxy, through an intermediary. Here man knows God through a proxy; and probably God too knows man through the same proxy. This proxy is the favoured individual, the privileged mediator,'[3]—i.e. the Son of God or the Last Prophet.

The second thing the Abrahamics did was to 'imprison' God in their finite time frame for their own political and temporal ends, making it clear that no higher forms of God can ever evolve through a pursuit of larger truths or deeper human insight and spiritual experience. The theory of evolution apparently does not apply to matters of faith. Consider Christianity and Christians. Even though they worship the Trinity and an abstract idea of the 'Father' God, it is the Son of God they really honour by making him co-equal with the Father God. The Father is now a figurehead, not a real God. It is his Son who rules. Not only that. Now that Jesus has been designated the Son of God, more Sons of God cannot be procreated in future by his Father. God's rights have been circumscribed by all-too-human ideologies masquerading as religions.

How can we claim God as omnipotent and eternal if He cannot evolve beyond what some desert cults imagined 2,000 or 1,400 years ago? Not only that, He cannot even send more Sons of God or Prophets to bring fresh ideas and spiritual perspectives for His earthly subjects. God is now in chains.

Another reason to consider the idea of the Abrahamic God as too narrow is this: God cannot be about politics. God becomes political when the idea transcends religious boundaries and seeks to impose Himself/Herself/Itself not only on willing believers but even on those who do not find the idea appealing.

Religion is about following a path to God; politics is about imposing a consensus view created by the elite on the whole population. Both Christianity and Islam want to fundamentally change the status quo on faith by insisting that theirs is the only way, and all others must ultimately agree to submit to their way of thinking.

This is no different from 'Godless Communism', which is about the *politics of the few* imposing itself on the *many* by claiming to represent the latter. Thus, numbers matter, and not the quality of those numbers.

Both Christianity and Islam (but not Judaism, which has this redeeming feature of not seeking to impose itself on the unwilling) are pursuing numbers like fast-moving consumer goods (FMCG) companies seek market share. How can this attempt be called religion by any stretch of imagination? This pursuit of religious market share would make Unilever or Procter & Gamble as worthy of religious faith as the two Abrahamic ones. If the reduction of God to an FMCG product is not debasement of the idea of God, then what is?

Now, let's come to this matter of freedom of religion. Where is the freedom in asserting that only my God is true and not others, when there is no proof of either? If God Himself/Herself is not free to evolve and reveal His/Her self as human imagination and capabilities improve, where is the freedom of religion here? It is stuck without hope in the past.

Also consider how Hinduism, Buddhism and Jainism look at the idea of God. Two of them even found that they can be moral and ethical without acknowledging a God, while Hinduism gives every individual the right to imagine and reimagine God in a way that suits their own svadharma, or core persona. Here, God serves the individual impartially, and is not subservient to some powerful church, mosque or denomination.

God empowers the individual, not the powerful multinational religious institutions preaching faith is truth, with no need for personal observation and experiential validation.

God in the Abrahamic tradition is eternally part of the earth-is-flat side of reasoning. God in the dharmic tradition is capable of scientific improvements, where we can go from earth-is-flat to earth-is-round to earth-is-shaped-like-an-imperfect-orange. Or, maybe, something else in the future, as more is learnt about it in the days to come.

In the Abrahamic tradition, God is bottled or stagnant water, not the fresh and clean stream that quenches our thirst and keeps moving along continuously. Freedom of religion is about an individual's right to make choices, not about the right of large and powerful religious multinationals seeking to hack the human mind and impose their own agendas.

Additionally, why is it necessary for any individual to buy the whole package and not just its good parts? For Mahatma Gandhi, Jesus's *Sermon on the Mount*—not much revered by many Christians even today—was a huge inspiration, and he adopted that part of Christianity as his own guiding principle. But Gandhi could remain a Hindu and seek Ram Rajya (Rule of Rama) at the same time. You may not agree with what he did, but did he not exercise his personal right to freedom of religion, which did not involve accepting all the other dogmas of an Abrahamic faith? Why buy the bathwater along with the baby?

In the Abrahamic world view, freedom of religion is about insisting that you buy the whole album of songs, most of which you may not like, instead of simply buying the one song you do. So, ask yourself again: what is true religion? And what is true freedom of religion?

The purpose of writing this book is to welcome Indians to a rediscovery of our dharmic nationhood and the dharmic nature of our peoples. Our nationhood is defined by a people who believe that there are higher truths to be learnt, not that all truths are already known and hence only need to be followed. I believe that our nationhood is defined by three ideals: one is that every individual has the right to seek an understanding of his or her relationship with the cosmos, with their fellow human beings and all living creatures in their own way. The idea of a unique God, discovered by a historical figure and defined by dogmas and scriptures, is not central to it. It is even antithetical to the idea of Bharat. A fixed or unchangeable idea about God or truth is incompatible with the idea of diversity and plurality, which are the hallmarks of a dharmic civilization. But if that is what you want to believe, so be it, as long as you do not seek to impose your ideas on a dharmic civilization. You need to follow your religion in a dharmic way.

Two, and this flows from the first proposition, whatever be your beliefs about God, or no God, about spirituality, or lack of it, you have the right to be respected. We are not a people who believe in the mere tolerance of different ideas and beliefs; we accept and even respect some of them, though we may sometimes argue frenetically against those ideas.

Freedom of thought, conscience, plurality and acceptance of differences are central to the varied ideas of dharma and a dharmic civilization.

Three, we do broadly believe in the theory of 'karma', which again is a concept on which there are better experts to consult. However, the two underlying thoughts behind the theory of karma are that it refers to action (usually right action) and that actions have consequences. Even though some people believe that the theory makes us fatalistic and willing to accept tyranny and injustices emanating from deeds in a previous birth, I believe that a more common sense meaning of the word is that what you do *now* will determine what will happen *later*. Your now is also partly the result of what you did earlier, though luck, random events and developments, and societal attitudes play a role in the cards you are dealt with. Karma, however, implies that you don't moan and groan about being dealt a poor hand. So, if you are poor and disadvantaged, it is your duty to focus on lifting yourself out of that poverty and not feel bitter about it endlessly; if you are rich, it is not just a reward for past good deeds but an incentive to do what is right going forward. Karma theory works best if we apply it prospectively to what we can do now, and references to past deeds only means accepting the reality that there are some things even we cannot change.

Dharma basically should mean making the best decisions depending on the circumstances we have been placed in in life, both as individuals and as a nation. This book is not an exploration of the idea of dharma but an attempt to link it to our ideas about India's nationhood as we go forward. We are a dharmic nation, and the more sharply we try to define this idea, the less successful we will be. The problem is that if you define an idea too tightly, it becomes practically theological in nature; it is best to leave the core of an idea a bit free and fluid around the edges, so that we can decide what it means in our context, in our life and in our attempt to define our nationhood.

I personally have no doubt that we are a dharmic nation, a dharmic civilization, and a Hindu Rashtra defined by diversity in culture and belief systems. We are not, and never should be, a theological state. This will inevitably lead to questions, even critiques, about what happens to Muslims and Christians, and whether this means majoritarianism is going to be the norm. I will surely attempt to answer them and debunk the doubts. For the purposes of this preface, suffice it to say that the so-called minorities, who are really global majorities, should not face any discrimination in Bharat, for Hinduism is not constructed on Abrahamic binaries. What they will face is a challenge to their narrow and exclusivist ideologies of unique and jealous gods, whose acceptance entails the denial of other ideas of God. No dharmic nation can survive if this binary is how Christianity and Islam choose to define themselves. But dharma can never be defeated by adharma, so Bharat will indeed prevail.

Another challenge to the idea of a dharmic nationhood is the so-called notion of civic nationalism. The problem lies in defining what it means beyond the idea of nationalism shorn of any ethnocentric roots. A Wikipedia definition of the term says: 'Civic nationalism, also known as liberal nationalism, is a form of nationalism identified by political philosophers who believe in an inclusive form of nationalism that adheres to traditional liberal values of freedom, tolerance, equality, individual rights and has no ethnocentrism.'

The web-based Wiktionary defines 'civic nationalism' as

'a political ideology which adheres to an inclusive form of national identity forged not by race or culture but support for classically liberal institutions and principles'.

There are four counters to these definitions, and the underlying assumption that a non-ethnocentric nation can be liberal and neutral to your identity is not necessarily true. If western woke liberalism is any guide, it is often about cancel culture, and slicing and dicing individuals into slots and hyphenated nationhood.

First, no nation is a *tabula rasa*, born with no historical memories. Woke liberalism is a direct outgrowth from European and American Christian experience, though in a secularized form. So, any laws made will have cultural biases already ingrained in the population that elects its legislators. American ideas of freedom of speech and religion are quite different from Indian, Islamic or even Chinese definitions of these terms. European ideas on gun control are different from those of America. In short, civic laws cannot be unrelated to inherited culture, whether this is overt or covert.

Second, civic nationalism will be impacted by how immigration and entry are controlled. The lesser the control, the greater the chance of different ideas of nationhood remaining long after a state has proclaimed itself to be ethnically neutral. Denmark and France found this out when their media published cartoons on the Prophet of Islam, and in retaliation, Muslims rioted and killed. Sweden found this out in April 2022 when immigrants, mostly Muslims, attacked policemen, leading the then prime minister, Magdalena Andersson, to exclaim: 'Segregation has been allowed to go so far that we have parallel societies in Sweden. We live in the same country but in completely different realities. We will have to reassess our previous truths and make tough decisions.'[4] In many European cities, there are no-go zones, comprising largely Muslim immigrant ghettos, for the police—a fact acknowledged by former German Chancellor Angela Merkel herself in a media interview in 2018.[5] So, no, civic nationalism cannot easily work in a state where immigration is liberally allowed.

Third, civic nationalism works best in less liberal or even autocratic countries. Examples are China, Marshal Josip Broz Tito's Yugoslavia, Communist Soviet Union or today's Singapore, where democratic freedoms are partly or fully sacrificed to keep social tensions contained and maintain reasonable equality before the law. Liberal, democratic societies will find it harder to maintain the rule of law if they also want to remain diverse and plural. The only exception may be Japan, which is ethnically monocultural, but then the price they pay is economic, by clamping down on immigration—hardly what a liberal society would want.

Fourth, there will always be tension between civic nationalism and regionalism or sub-nationalism. Let's take a supposedly ideal civic nationalist state like the Swiss Confederation, which is both democratic and sub-regional in its political structure. The 26 cantons can do their own thing, have their own constitutions, courts and laws, subject only to some common obligations to the central laws. What this essentially means is that each canton is a nation in itself, and the cantons together can overturn a national law. In 2009, a referendum on allowing or disallowing minarets in mosques was decisively won by conservative voters, overturning a national elite consensus opposing the ban.

The Guardian reported: 'The [referendum] result also represented an act of mass defiance of the national establishment. The government, mainstream political parties, the churches, the main newspapers, the national president, the powerful business lobby, and the Vatican all opposed the ban, but it was backed by 22 of the country's 26 cantons on a national turnout of more than 53%.'[6]

Put another way, a coalition of voters in cantons can choose not to be 'secular' or neutral as defined normally. It is driven by its own historical and linguistic chauvinisms.

The civic nationalism model is yet to prove itself as a viable idea of inclusive statehood or governance anywhere in the world. The idea of dharmic nationhood, with enough vagueness around its edges, is what may work for India that is Bharat.

Lastly, the reason for touting the idea of a dharmic nationhood or Hindu Rashtra is the abject failure of secularism in India. Secularism originally meant maintaining equidistance between religions, or equal treatment of individuals and religious institutions by the state, but it has become a cruel joke. Hinduism has borne the brunt of this bad idea, formulated in a European context, and mangled out of shape in India. Secularism has often meant minoritarianism, or special treatment to minorities. It is even partly Hinduphobic, as interventions in Hindu beliefs, rituals and practices have been burnt into the Constitution in the name of abolishing 'casteism'. Thus, state interventions, most of it with adverse consequences for Hindu religious rights, have neutered the constitutional guarantees of religious freedoms to all communities. It has also damaged minority rights, for Muslims have tended to demand religious rights, and were thus short-changed on economic rights, education and social change.

This negativity to Hindu religious freedoms and protection

of Hindu rights cannot be undone without an explicit commitment to dharmic nationhood or a Hindu Rashtra. That is the core of the argument in this book.

A note: this book was not written as a book. It was written in stages, as events unfolded themselves over the last decade. Most of these thoughts evolved with time, and mark my own journey from secularism to dharmic thinking. It is thus a work in progress.

1

A UNIQUE PLURALIST IDEA UNDER ATTACK

India is unique. Its uniqueness stems from the fact that it is only one of two global civilizations (the other being Chinese) with an unbroken history of nearly five millennia, even after being impacted by two colonialisms, one Islamic and the other British.[1] The Egyptian, Sumerian, Mayan, Greek, Roman and other ancient civilizations—to name just a few of the significant ones—have disappeared or shrunk. Traditional African religions and cultures, too, are dying under the assaults of proselytizing faiths. But Indian culture is still around. Hopefully, it is in the process of reinvention and rejuvenation.

India's uniqueness stems from the fact that it spawned four major religions—Hinduism, Buddhism, Jainism and Sikhism—mostly without the rancour and bloodshed seen in Abrahamic faiths. These four have been complemented by several other spiritual and cultural traditions (aka *sampradayas*), some of which we today call 'tribal' or *vanvasi* (non-urban or forest dwellers). These religious and ethical ideas, philosophies, traditions, rituals and practices interacted with one another, debated and contested among themselves, occasionally even indulged in some violence, but ultimately learnt to coexist and co-evolve. This synthesis is what we call dharmic, even Hindu, a culture of diversity and accepted difference that goes beyond tolerance, and whose definition transcends the conventional meaning of 'religion'. It is a civilization whose core tenets are blurry, but the broad contours are clear: it is about each one finding their own path to higher truths, to elevated spiritual realms, or even discarding the idea of God or religion and instead opting for a code of ethical conduct that transcends religion (as in Buddhism, for example). This culture did not have a problem with those who did not believe in any particular idea of God or religion, or didn't accept the authority of the Vedas or the Upanishads (the Charvakas or Nastiks, for example). But the idea that actions have consequences, i.e. the theory of karma, is accepted by most Indic traditions.

India stands out because its mainstream religion, Hinduism, did not have a recognized founder, or a set of scriptural fundamentals and an all-encompassing 'holy book'. It is a culture that evolved from the ground up, not descending from the heavens above. Even though the Vedas are said to be divinely revealed *shruti*s (that which is heard), and large parts of the shlokas and mantras we recite even today in our religious ceremonies and rituals emanate from there (or the Upanishads linked to them), the bulk of Hindu, Buddhist, Jain and Sikh sacred literature falls in the category called *smriti*s (texts attributed to exalted human minds). Most important, there is no obligation to believe in an Abrahamic binary, where it is either my God or the devil, a true believer in the one true religion, or a kafir (disbeliever).

India also made the transition from a diverse pagan

culture to one that developed a high level of philosophical, metaphysical and spiritual sophistication unknown in the ancient world. Among pagan cultures, only India managed to transcend the limitations imposed by tribalism and developed a soft power that is envied by more powerful religions even today. Yoga, meditation and Ayurveda are just three examples of the Indic soft power that the world wants to capture and claim as its own.

Our uniqueness also lies in the fact that roughly 90 per cent of the people who are grouped under the label 'Hindu' live in one geography, a country called India, which is actually a truncated version of the land we called Bharat, which extended from Afghanistan to Myanmar, and from the Himalayas to the peninsular region of southern India, where the three seas (the Indian Ocean, the Arabian Sea and the Bay of Bengal) meet. The world's third-largest religion, with approximately 1.2 billion people, according to the World Population Review,[2] is unique because it is physically in one place and must plough a lonely furrow when fighting for its rights.

Thus, while the Pew Research Center counts 158 Christian-majority countries and territories (as of 2011),[3] and 51 Muslim-majority ones (as of 2020),[4] Hindus have only three: Nepal (81 per cent), India (80 per cent) and Mauritius (56 per cent).[5] The exact numbers may vary due to how majorities are counted, and also because of religious conflicts that continue in some states and which may yet create new religious majorities after bifurcation. For example, Sudan was a Muslim-majority country till it split into two, with the southern part becoming a Christian-majority state in 2011. The Christian Timor-Leste (East Timor) was part of Muslim-majority Indonesia till it split as a separate state in 1999. But there is little doubt that there are over 150 Christian-majority countries and over 50 Muslim ones in the world today.

The upshot: if anything happens to Muslims or Christians in India, the world gets to know and make a fuss about it; if worse things happen to Hindus anywhere, it is barely acknowledged. Even as this introductory chapter was being written in June 2022, as if to prove this point, almost all Islamic countries were outraging and hauling India over the coals for a negative reference to the Prophet of Islam by a Bharatiya Janata Party (BJP) spokesperson, Nupur Sharma, who was emotionally reacting to derogatory references to the Shiva Lingam on social media and elsewhere.[6] Blasphemy, they shouted, without noting the hypocrisy of not acknowledging what had happened before that. In 2014–15, a few stray incidents involving vandalism or theft in some of Delhi's churches were blown out of proportion in the mainstream media as an attack on the faith, but records with the Delhi Police have shown that '206 temples, 30 gurdwaras and three churches (out of some 200 or more churches in Delhi) and 14 mosques were burgled in 2014'.[7]

However, this is an aside, and we would be amiss if we did not acknowledge that there is also a downside to India's uniqueness—at least two of them, in fact. Today we call it 'caste' even though the word is Portuguese in origin, and what we call the 'caste system' was something that congealed into a curse under colonial rule. Like every other society, India had (and continues to have) social groups, what we call jatis, but we also had a loosely constructed idea of hierarchy, called varna, which was given an ideological shape in the *Manu-smriti*, or Laws of Manu. In this hierarchy, the Brahmin is at the top, followed by the Kshatriya, the Vaishya and the Shudra. The absolute underclass, those involved in despised or degrading work, were deemed untouchable.

As a scriptural text, the casteism that stares us in the face in *Manu-smriti* is no worse than some of the negative exhortations in the Bible or the Koran, but modern-day politics has given *Manu-smriti*—a human composition—the stature of an albatross hanging around Hindu necks. Whenever Hindus seek to take pride in their heritage, *Manu-smriti* and caste are waved in front of their faces, and they are told that there is no such thing as Hinduism. There is only caste, caste and caste, and caste is about discrimination and oppression. But whatever the reason for caste becoming such a calcified institution, there is little doubt that we have to deal with it as a given. While jatis provide communities with social capital and supportive relationships, the inherent assumption that varna and jati are both hierarchical and oppressive needs demolition and substantial reform. We are on that road, but nowhere near where we need to be.

The second uniqueness that we should consider a problem is the colonized nature of our discourse—led by our elite, who appear to have swallowed western critiques of Hinduism hook, line and sinker. Many among our English-speaking elites are self-loathing Hindus, and 'secularism' is the stick used to berate or downplay what is a uniquely Hindu heritage. Thomas Babington Macaulay, the British historian now famous (or rather infamous) for his 'Minute on English Education', written in the mid-1830s, urged the then Governor-General Lord William Bentinck to abolish traditional Indian education in Sanskrit and Persian and replace it with English. The idea was to 'form a class who may be interpreters between us [i.e. the British], and the millions whom we govern—a class of persons Indian in blood and colour, but English in taste, in opinions, in morals and in intellect'.[8]

Nobody can doubt that some of Macaulay's intentions were indeed good and intended to bring the latest in science and literature to Indians, but underlying it all was the racist notion of 'the White man's burden' and the lack of knowledge of what were the better parts of India's heritage. Just as Macaulay was probably right to suggest that India was lacking in modern knowledge, he was dead wrong in believing that our ancient literature and languages contained nothing of worth.

Macaulay was successful beyond his wildest dreams, and, to this day, many Indian institutions, from the judiciary to the police to the civil service, are run like they were in colonial times. Worse, English is now the only language of aspiration for the young and restless in India, much to the detriment of Indian regional languages. India is ruled by an English-speaking elite, even if many of them speak poor English, and who send their children to study abroad even as they let our own education system rot into irrelevance. This elite, largely uprooted from its heritage, looks at India and Hinduism as regressive and not worth saving.

No group typifies this attitude better than the Indian Left, which draws all its working hypotheses from European history and Marxist literature. That Karl Marx wrote about India without ever setting foot on this land does not matter to them. But Marx's racist attitude—which saw British colonialism as a disruptive, but ultimately modernizing, influence on India—is indirectly reflected in how Marxist intellectuals and historians read India's past and the present.

Marx was critical of the East India Company's despotism in India, but he saw the disruption as bringing about a revolution by accident. He wrote in the *New York Herald Tribune* on 10 June 1853:

> England, it is true, in causing a social revolution in Hindostan, was actuated only by the vilest interests, and was stupid in her manner of enforcing them. But that is not the question. The question is, can mankind fulfil its destiny without a fundamental revolution in the social state of Asia? If not, whatever may have been the crimes of England she was the unconscious tool of history in bringing about that revolution.[9]

The wholesale rewriting of Indian history by leftists from the late 1960s onwards, when Indira Gandhi made her fateful alliance with the communists to remain in power, resulted in towering historians of the pre- and post-Independence era, including R.C. Majumdar, K.A. Nilakanta Sastri and Jadunath Sarkar, among several others, being called 'communal'. History was often rewritten by the Left with no knowledge of Sanskrit or regional languages, or any understanding of India's sacred literature.

However, with the rise of new writers with a better understanding of Indian heritage, the deracinated 'secular' intellectual is gradually being questioned on their competence to write, or even rewrite history. But the task of undermining rooted Indian scholarship has now been taken up in earnest by western academicians. Eurocentric writing is now the preserve not only of colonial European institutions but post-colonial American academia too, and almost all major historical research on India is now being done in the United States (US).

A curious alliance of the global Left and Right, and deracinated Indian liberals, who have bought into the idea that Hindu culture is largely worthless or even evil, is now seeking to undermine whatever little we can take pride in as

Hindus and as upholders of dharma, the eternal but always evolving global and cosmic order.

The new attacks on Hinduism are thus mostly foreign in origin, supported by co-opted Indians who have now been given an international stage to air their grievances.

In September 2021, Hinduphobic, Hindumisic or Hindu-sceptic academicians in the US organized a three-day virtual discussion on how to 'Dismantle Global Hindutva'.[10] They apparently had the support of over 40 US universities, though some institutions did indeed distance themselves from the event. The pamphlet and online publicity material announcing the event featured a row of Rashtriya Swayamsevak Sangh (RSS) volunteers represented as nails, with the clawing side of an inverted communist hammer being used to remove them from the woodwork. The resultant blowback on this dehumanized way of depicting people forced the organizers to change the visual, but it did not prevent the event from being staged or detract them from their primary goal of using fault lines within Hindu society to put the community, both in the US and worldwide, on the defensive.[11]

In the weeks before the discussion forum was organized, Hindus in Rutgers University had asked the administration to restrain a few Hindu-bashing professors, such as Audrey Truschke, from stigmatizing Hinduism and Hindus. Truschke, among other things, wrote a book titled *Aurangzeb: The Man and the Myth*, which sought to whitewash the religious bigotry of the seventeenth-century Mughal emperor Aurangzeb.[12]

But the university chose to treat this as part of academic freedom. Earlier, Truschke had faced considerable criticism and anger from Hindus in India and elsewhere when she claimed that Sita had indirectly referred to Shri Rama as a 'misogynistic pig' for making her go through an *agnipariksha* (trial by fire) after she was rescued from Lanka. But some scholars of the Ramayana were appalled with her choice of words.[13] In a wholly negative essay on the Mahabharata, Truschke wrote that the epic 'rationalises mass slaughter'.[14]

Earlier, a Hindu student elected to the Oxford University Student Union, Rashmi Samant, was hounded out of her post by a cabal ferreting out some unfortunate statements made by her on Twitter,[15] and which she had disowned, to paint her as a Hindu fanatic.

Earlier, a petition signed by 44,000 people had demanded the sacking of a postdoctoral researcher at New College, Dr Abhijit Sarkar, alleging that he was guilty of 'criminal and racist hate speech'.[16] In one deleted Instagram post, Dr Sarkar had apparently even boasted that he had broken several Saraswati idols as a child 'by smashing them on the floor'.[17] The details of the Oxford investigation into his conduct, still under wraps at the time of writing, appear to have vindicated Samant, but the details were not disclosed.[18]

In 2015–16, the University of California, Irvine, rejected two endowment chairs worth $3 million that were sponsored by a US non-profit, Dharma Civilization Foundation (DCF) to research and lecture on Vedic and Indic civilizations, Modern India, Jainism and Sikhism at the university. A committee set up to take a relook at the offer after a protest by some students and academics rejected it. It claimed that the DCF was 'unusually explicit and prescriptive on appropriate disciplinary formations, what constitutes good or acceptable scholarship, and, indeed, what constitutes good or acceptable scholars' to justify its decision.[19] But there is little doubt that it was the DCF's linkages with the RSS and the US-based Hindu Swayamsevak Sangh that were the real reasons for the rejection.

In April 2021, the Hindu American Foundation (HAF), a Hindu advocacy group in the US, was targeted through media articles for being linked to groups that allegedly indulged in 'slow genocide' of Muslims and Christians in India. The foundation and four other US organizations received $833,000 in Covid-19 relief funding from the US government to keep workers on their payrolls during the pandemic. These articles claimed that the HAF and the other four were linked to Hindu supremacist and religious groups.[20]

Apart from the HAF, the four organizations mentioned were Vishwa Hindu Parishad of America, Ekal Vidyalaya Foundation of USA, Infinity Foundation and Sewa International, a Hindu faith-based charity.

The HAF chose to sue Truschke, two founder-members of an organization called Hindus for Human Rights, an executive director of the Indian American Muslim Council and the North America chairman of the Federation of Indian American Christian Organizations for defamation in the United States District Court for the District of Columbia. The HAF has said that such attacks, based on alleged closeness to Hindutva groups, could not be ignored since it was affecting donors' willingness to fund it.[21]

Sewa International, which has been similarly targeted and is concerned about future funding, describes itself on its website as:

> [A] Hindu faith-based, humanitarian, nonprofit service organization registered under Internal Revenue Code 501 (c) (3). Founded in 2003, Sewa International is part of a larger movement that started in India in 1989 and is active in twenty countries. Sewa serves humanity irrespective of race, color, religion, gender or nationality.

> We specialize in disaster relief and rehabilitation. Our development programs focus on family services; child, tribal and refugee welfare; women empowerment; health; and education. In addition to our work in the US, we have undertaken development projects in Colombia, Guyana, India, Kenya, Pakistan and Sri Lanka.[22]

The purpose of going into some length about these incidents, events and issues is this: there is a concerted attack against many things Hindu in several academic institutions in the West, and it is difficult to believe that all this is merely the result of scholarly work and opinion. Most likely, Hindu organizations in the US are being targeted because they can be a source of funding and support for Hindus in India in the same way Christian evangelical organizations use dollar funding to pursue their conversion agendas in India.

In part, this ability of Hinduphobes and Hinduism-sceptics to demonize Hindu groups and organizations is the result of some confusion created by offhand utterances of the latter. The election of Narendra Modi as prime minister with an absolute majority of his own in India's parliament in 2014 has given rise to a lot of loose talk among his supporters and Hindu groups about establishing a Hindu Rashtra, about the ideology of Hindutva and 'Hindu nationalism'. Add some elements of violence by cow-protection groups against Muslims and it becomes incredibly easy to give the dog a bad name and hang it. After a few lynchings shocked the nation, some members of India's 'secular' media even called India 'lynchistan'.[23]

Many opposition politicians have now mainstreamed the idea that Hinduism is different from Hindutva, the latter being shorthand for political Hinduism, Islamophobia and violent assertion of 'majoritarian' and 'Hindu-supremacist' ideas.

This is what one of India's most erudite members of Parliament, Shashi Tharoor, who represents the Thiruvananthapuram constituency in the Lok Sabha as a member of the Congress party, does in his writings, including a book titled *Why I Am a Hindu*. As I noted in a review of the book in *Swarajya* magazine,[24] Tharoor has diametrically opposite views on Hinduism and Hindutva, which loosely translated, means 'Hindu-ness'. In Tharoor's view, Hinduism is a pluralist, inclusivist and open-minded belief system of Hindus, while Hindutva is violent, exclusive and anti-minorities. To be sure, Vinayak Damodar 'Veer' Savarkar, who popularized the word 'Hindutva', actually gave this wide definition to Hindutva, not Hinduism, which we shall discuss later.

In the review of Tharoor's book, I wrote:

> Tharoor's demonisation of Hindutva focuses on weaving violent fringe groups, the loose cannons in the Sangh Parivar, and communal incidents since Independence, and especially 2002, into one quilt of intolerance. Just as some Hindu partisans would like to reduce all of Islam to jihadi Islam, Tharoor does the same hit-job on political Hinduism. He traces all of it to an ideology which was first crafted by Veer Savarkar, expanded on by Guru M S Golwalkar, the Rashtriya Swayamsevak Sangh's (RSS) second chief, and given political shape by one of the Jana Sangh's founders, Deendayal Upadhyaya.
>
> The Bharatiya Janata Party (BJP) of today is the inheritor of all three streams of thought, though one can hardly call today's political Hindutva of the BJP as being anywhere close to the radical ideology

> envisioned by Savarkar. In his own time, Savarkar was disillusioned by the pusillanimity of the Sangh, and he would probably see today's BJP as a namby-pamby outfit unfit to call itself a party espousing Hindutva. But to Tharoor it does not matter, since the idea is to smear political Hinduism with the blood-lust of those Muslim-hating vigilante groups that have crept out of the woodwork, possibly emboldened by the rise of the BJP to power in many states. So, to restate the obvious: Tharoor's declaration of his Hindu-ness, or Hindutva, is largely polemical.[25]

The irony is that Hindutva is a much better descriptor of what Hindus are about than even the term 'Hinduism', as there was no specific religion that called itself 'Hinduism' before colonial interventions. It was colonial description that saw the collection of traditions, rituals, beliefs, practices and revered texts as Hinduism, a religion like Christianity or Islam, but simply not as good. Some academics who have sought to decolonize the social sciences, such as Emeritus Prof. (Dr) S.N. Balagangadhara of Ghent University, Belgium, suggest that 'even when taken together (these Indic beliefs and practices) do not constitute a religion that can be structurally unified as Hinduism...'[26] In his book, *What Does It Mean to Be 'Indian'?* written in collaboration with Sarika Rao, Prof. Balagangadhara claims that 'Hinduism, the phenomenon constructed by our colonial masters, is an experiential entity to them, but not to us. In this sense, Hinduism is not a part of Indian culture. It has no existence outside the colonial experience of India.'[27]

Prof. Balagangadhara would be in a minority among academicians and ordinary Indians today, who would not go about denying that there is something called Hinduism even if the umbrella term was invented or popularized during the British colonial era. Sometimes, a thing that does not exist in theory becomes a reality by constant assumptions about it. Also, just as a child is given a name by its parents rather than asked to choose its own, people and nations are often not defined by how they see themselves, but how others see them. 'India', 'Hindus' and 'Hinduism' are derivatives of the word 'Sindhu', the Indus River. People living on the other side of the river were described by ancient Persians as Hindus, with the letter 'S' being replaced by 'H' in Persian. So, yes, 'Hinduism' may well have been coined by the colonialists, but we now own the term, thank you.

However, the larger point is this: that there were Hindus cannot be denied. That there was a specific religion called Hinduism can be questioned. But Hindutva, the idea of being Hindu even without a construct called Hinduism, is more difficult to deny. That Hindutva may have a political dimension does not mean something called Hindu-ness does not exist. It does.

So, how does this need arise among Indologists, western academicians and Left-liberal intellectuals to demonize Hindutva and also those who have banded together under this banner, including the much-maligned Sangh Parivar?

The Sangh Parivar, which includes over 30 affiliated or loosely linked front organizations, including mass-based ones like the Vishwa Hindu Parishad, the Akhil Bharatiya Vidyarthi Parishad and the Bharatiya Mazdoor Sangh, not to speak of the world's largest political party, the BJP, which in May 2022 completed eight uninterrupted years in power at the Centre, is not centrally controlled. Its front organizations and affiliates are autonomous in what they do, and, in many ways, mirror the huge diversities in Hindu culture itself. The Sangh is neither a religious nor a political conglomerate, but its actions impact several aspects of society. To quote Ratan Sharda, a lifelong swayamsevak, from his book, *Conflict Resolution: The RSS Way*, the Sangh 'defines Hindutva as the essence of the Hindu character of Bharat, ie India. This essence is pluralism, respect for all faiths and views, respect for nature, belief in *karma* and rebirth, treating the nation as motherland and viewing unity in diversity'.[28]

The Sangh differentiates between nation and state, and its concept of *rashtra* does not mean state, which can be secular and respect all religions. It also does not conflate the idea of dharma with religion, which is correct from all definitional points of view among scholars, though dharma does include some aspects that which can be called religion. In Sanskrit, dharma means that which 'upholds' society and the cosmos. The RSS itself is not a religious organization but still holds Hindu culture to be its theme song.

This brings me to the purpose of this book, which is largely an aggregation of articles I have written for *Swarajya* over the last few years. (Some of these articles are reproduced as first published in *Swarajya* or its website [www.swarajyamag.com], some after modifications, and some only in part with major changes.) Some of these articles have been merged under a broader theme.

The purpose of putting together these many articles, written at various points of time over the last seven years, into a more comprehensive whole is to make a simple point: if India is to claim its 'tryst with destiny', to use Jawaharlal Nehru's evocative words, it needs to rediscover its heritage in terms that are at once modern and relevant to today's concerns. If Hindu Rashtra has to have a meaning beyond the narrow-mindedness that the term seems to conjure up in the minds of the 'secular' individual, it needs a clearer definition and inclusiveness.

However, inclusiveness cannot mean blind acceptance of Abrahamic ideas of universalism, which are essentially about exclusivity and forced uniformity. Given the sheer diversity of the Indian social and religious evolution over centuries, the term 'Hindu Rashtra' means a dharmic nation, a civilization that lives by the ideal of unity without uniformity, diversity without divisiveness. It needs a certain amount of debunking of Abrahamic creedal values, which claim superiority over other ideas and ideals.

The purpose of a dharmic nation is to universalize inclusivity without submerging real or subliminal identities, which is exactly what our historical experience suggests. India is a dharmic nation, which you can also call Hindu Rashtra, where the term 'Hindu' is cultural rather than religious. Veer Savarkar got it right with the term 'Hindutva', which is also not related to the religion we call Hinduism. It is about loyalty and fidelity to this country and its people. And a call to celebrate its heritage without assuming that there was some Golden Age that we need to recreate today.

The focus points of this book are threefold. One is to expand on the idea of Hindu Rashtra as a dharmic nation and debunk the presumption that it is about establishing a theocratic state; two, we will list the challenges facing our dharmic society as it seeks to assert itself in India and globally; and three, we will enunciate the basis on which the two proselytizing religions—Christianity and Islam—can integrate themselves into the idea of Bharat that is India, and without losing their core identities. They can become dharmic faiths too.

2

ARE HINDU RASHTRA AND HINDUTVA NARROW CONCEPTS?

One problem with the idea of a Hindu Rashtra is that it is simply undefined as an idea or an ideal. Those who want one are not clear on what a Hindu Rashtra would mean for the citizens of India. Those who are against the idea are not sure why they dislike it, as I wrote in mid-2020.[1] Using loaded terms such as 'majoritarianism' or 'Hindu fundamentalism' to oppose the idea is simply a form of negative labelling. It helps opponents of the idea to demonize it, both by linking the worst behaviours of some Hindus or Hindu organizations, or by summarily rejecting it, as it would mean India becoming a 'Hindu Pakistan'[2]—a theocratic state that defines itself too narrowly and uses violence to impose religious ideas on the whole population, which may not be so inclined.

In one of his columns for *Hindustan Times*, Vir Sanghvi, one of India's best writers in English, including on the subject of food, challenged the votaries of Hindu Rashtra to give us a 'what-if' book[3] on what India would have been like if it had really become a Hindu Rashtra in 1947. In some ways, this book, parts of which were written long before Sanghvi asked for it, is an attempt to answer his questions and the critics of a future Hindu Rashtra.

Among other things, Sanghvi points out the problems India would have faced if it had defined itself as a Hindu Rashtra. Among the questions he throws at those who believe in the idea of a Hindu Rashtra are the following: what would Partition have been like? (That is, would we have had more two-way religious migrations if India had declared itself a Hindu Rashtra in 1947 itself?) What kind of government would we have had? Would we ever have had a claim to Kashmir? Would we have followed a radically different ideology? Would minorities be second-class citizens in a Hindu Rashtra? What about the Northeast? What about the Sikhs? What would happen to caste? Where's the book explaining what a Hindu Rashtra would look like?[4]

Some of these questions reveal what India's 'secular' intellectuals think when what they really want to ask is: what would have happened to us liberal elites if India had become a Hindu Rashtra on 15 August 1947? Some questions cannot be answered, for the answers depend on the policies adopted. Babasaheb Ambedkar, for example, wanted a controlled exchange of populations because he suspected Muslims of having divided loyalties.[5] But whether two-way migrations would have actually followed, as they did in Punjab, is a difficult question to answer, since it is highly unlikely that people would have abandoned their land and properties for an uncertain future on the other side of the border. (In fact, this was the case in East Pakistan [present-day Bangladesh], where the migrations have been going on for decades in dribs and drabs, even to this day.)

What kind of government would a Hindu Rashtra have

had? Actually, we know the answer to this, for, despite Nehru, in the first 15 years after Partition, India did not show any disdain for its Hindu heritage. As Subramanian Swamy, a BJP Rajya Sabha Member of Parliament (MP), pointed out in his book, *The Ideology of India's Modern Right*, most of India's first institutions had emblems using Hindu or dharmic motifs and messages, such as the four lions on the Ashoka pillar (the motto being *Satyameva Jayate*), the Armed Forces (*Sewa Paramo Dharma*), the Supreme Court (*Yato Dharmastato Jayah*), the spy arm Research and Analysis Wing (*Dharmo Rakshati Rakshitah*) or even the Life Insurance Corporation (*Yogakshemam Vahamyaham*).[6] The original copy of the Constitution of India carried pictures of Hindu gods and Hindu motifs.[7]

The commitment to plurality and diversity is a defining feature of Hinduism and not just a gift of our Constitution, and hence there was no reason to think we would have built a theocracy. The fact that Hindu and Indic themes found a place in the original copy of the Constitution only suggests that the writers took this for granted. As for Kashmir, the terms of Partition were clear: the state's accession depended on the ruler's choice, and the choice of the Maharaja of Kashmir was to sign up with India. Sikhs would always have had a space in India, for the separation of Sikhism from Hinduism was a gradual process, and the two communities have always had a close relationship (described best by the phrase '*roti beti ka rishta*', meaning intermarriage and joint dining). As for the Northeast, it would have been no different from what it is now politically, with greater autonomy for some states and more integrative linkages with others.

Sanghvi has, however, done a service to Hindus who demand Hindu Rashtra by asking these questions. But, as we shall see, these are not questions emerging only because a 'Hindu Nationalist' BJP came to power in 2014. Many of them were raised as far back as in the 1940s, including by Ambedkar in his monograph on Pakistan, where he agreed with Mohammed Ali Jinnah that Muslims were a separate nation. Using nineteenth-century French historian and philosopher Ernest Renan's definition of what constitutes a nation, Ambedkar asked rhetorically: 'Is it or is it not a fact that Muslims of India are an exclusive group? Is it or is it not a fact that they have a consciousness of [a] kind? Is it or is it not a fact that every Muslim is possessed by a longing to belong to his own group and not any non-Muslim group?'[8]

He also pointed out what he thought was the illogic in Savarkar's own definition of Hindu Rashtra and Hindutva, and how Muslims should be treated in an undivided India.

The funny thing is he did not raise these questions about other minorities like Christians, even though Christianity is motivated by similar exclusivist impulses. Over the last two decades, we have seen Christian southern Sudan separated from Muslim Sudan; Cyprus was divided along religious lines; largely Christian East Timor got independence from Muslim Indonesia. In India, the Christian-majority states of the Northeast have always nursed a separatist streak, often aided by the church.

Partition or no Partition, the questions raised by Ambedkar, and now Sanghvi, cannot be ducked any more. It would be apt to begin the discussion on Hindu Rashtra by first dealing with the Ambedkar–Savarkar disagreement in the 1940s. Ambedkar pointed out, not unfairly, that both Jinnah and Savarkar agreed that Hindus and Muslims were separate nations and the only question was whether the country should be divided along religious lines or function separately within the same unified state.[9]

It is worth quoting Ambedkar's criticism of Savarkar's position at some length, especially his conclusions. He writes:

> Strange as it may appear, Mr Savarkar and Mr Jinnah, instead of being opposed to each other on the one nation versus two nations issue, are in complete agreement about it. Both agree, not only agree but insist, that there are two nations in India—one the Muslim nation and the other the Hindu nation. They differ only as regards the terms and conditions on which the two nations should live. Mr Jinnah says India should be cut up into two, Pakistan and Hindustan, the Muslim nation to occupy Pakistan and the Hindu nation to occupy Hindustan. Mr Savarkar, on the other hand, insists that, although there are two nations in India, India shall not be divided into two parts, one for Muslims and the other for the Hindus; that the two nations shall dwell in one country and shall live under the mantle of one single constitution; that the constitution shall be such that the Hindu nation will be enabled to occupy a predominant position that is due to it and the Muslim nation made to live in the position of subordinate cooperation with the Hindu nation. In the struggle for political power between the two nations the rule of the game which Mr Savarkar prescribes is to be one-man-one-vote, be the man Hindu or Muslim. In his scheme a Muslim is to have no advantage which a Hindu does not have. Minority is to be no justification for privilege and majority is to be no ground for penalty. The state will guarantee the Muslims any defined measure of political power in the

> form of Muslim religion and Muslim culture. But the state will not guarantee secured seats in the legislature or in the administration and, if such guarantee is insisted upon by the Muslims, such guaranteed quota is not to exceed their proportion to the general population. Thus, by confiscating its weightages, Mr Savarkar would even strip the Muslim nation of all the political privileges it has secured so far.[10]

Ambedkar praises Savarkar's position as bold and clear, something the Congress wanted to obfuscate.

He writes:

> This alternative of Mr Savarkar to Pakistan has about it a frankness, boldness and definiteness which distinguishes it from the irregularity, vagueness and indefiniteness which characterizes the Congress declarations about minority rights. Mr Savarkar's scheme has at least the merit of telling the Muslims, thus far and no further. The Muslims know where they are with regard to the Hindu Maha Sabha. On the other hand, with the Congress the Musalmans find themselves nowhere because the Congress has been treating the Muslims and the minority question as a game in diplomacy, if not in duplicity.

But Ambedkar is scathing in his rebuttal of Savarkar's idea of a unified India, where both Hindus and Muslims lived as separate entities. He said this was illogical, inconsistent and even 'dangerous' for the new country.

He wrote:

> At the same time, it must be said that Mr Savarkar's attitude is illogical, if not queer. Mr Savarkar admits that the Muslims are a separate nation. He concedes that they

> have a right to cultural autonomy. He allows them to have a national flag. Yet he opposes the demand of the Muslim nation for a separate national home. If he claims a national home for the Hindu nation, how can he refuse the claim of the Muslim nation for a national home?
>
> It would not have been a matter of much concern if inconsistency was the only fault of Mr Savarkar. But Mr Savarkar in advocating his scheme is really creating a most dangerous situation for the safety and security of India. History records two ways as being open to a major nation to deal with a minor nation when they are citizens of the same country and are subject to the same constitution. *One way is to destroy the nationality of the minor nation and to assimilate and absorb it into the major nation, so as to make one nation out of two. This is done by denying to the minor nation any right to language, religion or culture and by seeking to enforce upon it the language, religion and culture of the major nation* [emphasis added]. The other way is to divide the country and to allow the minor nation a separate, autonomous and sovereign existence, independent of the major nation. Both these ways were tried in Austria and Turkey, the second after the failure of the first.

The above paragraph suggests that when two 'nations'—a term defined by Renan—live in one territory, it needs violence and coercion to create one nation out of two. Ambedkar thus criticizes Savarkar for being wishy-washy about his idea of a Hindu India.

Ambedkar continued:

> Mr. Savarkar adopts neither of these two ways. He does not propose to suppress the Muslim nation. On the

> contrary he is nursing and feeding it by allowing it to retain its religion, language and culture, elements which go to sustain the soul of a nation. At the same time, he does not consent to divide the country so as to allow the two nations to become separate, autonomous states, each sovereign in its own territory. He wants the Hindus and the Muslims to live as two separate nations in one country, each maintaining its own religion, language and culture. One can understand and even appreciate the wisdom of the theory of suppression of the minor nation by the major nation because the ultimate aim is to bring into being one nation. But one cannot follow what advantage a theory has which says that there must ever be two nations but that there shall be no divorce between them. One can justify this attitude only if the two nations were to live as partners in friendly intercourse with mutual respect and accord. *But that is not to be, because Mr. Savarkar will not allow the Muslim nation to be co-equal in authority with the Hindu nation. He wants the Hindu nation to be the dominant nation and the Muslim nation to be the servient nation* [emphasis added]. Why Mr. Savarkar, after sowing this seed of enmity between the Hindu nation and the Muslim nation, should want that they should live under one constitution and occupy one country, is difficult to explain.

However, while Ambedkar is right to point out Savarkar's inconsistencies and contradictory logic, one should also question what he himself was advocating: basically, he was saying that a nation can be forged only through violence (see sentences in italics above), and thus a Hindu Rashtra could have come into being only by suppressing Muslims and their sense of nationhood.

In many ways, thus, Ambedkar was not only more extreme than Savarkar on the Muslim question but also off the mark. His views came entirely from Renan's definition of 'nation', which is rooted in the idea of a people with a common memory of joint struggles and staying in a well-defined geographical area that is defensible and separate. In short, this is the Abrahamic, Westphalian idea of the nation-state that evolved in Christian Western Europe, and where geography aided such nationalisms.

Renan said:

> A nation is a soul, a spiritual principle. Two things, which in truth are but one, constitute this soul or spiritual principle. One lies in the past, one in the present. One is the possession in common of a rich legacy of memories; the other is present-day consent, the desire to live together, the will to perpetuate the value of the heritage that one has received in an undivided form... The nation, like the individual, is the culmination of a long past of endeavours, sacrifice, and devotion. Of all cults, that of the ancestors is the most legitimate, for the ancestors have made us what we are. A heroic past, great men, glory (by which I understand genuine glory), this is the social capital upon which one bases a national idea. To have common glories in the past and to have a common will in the present; to have performed great deeds together, to wish to perform still more—these are the essential conditions for being a people. One loves in proportion to the sacrifices to which one has consented, and in proportion to the ills that one has suffered. One loves the house that one has built and that one has handed down.[11]

In India, several 'nations' (as defined by Renan) have existed in the same state, and several 'states' have existed separately but whose people have shared a common sense of 'nationality'. Here, nationality is defined as sharing a common cultural sensibility and a shared sense of 'a sacred geography' (which is the title of a book by Diana L. Eck on India). India's sense of nationhood is civilizational in character rather than a Renan equivalent of the nation-state.

Looked at more closely, Savarkar's sense of a unified India dominated politically by Hindus is not as outrageous as it seems. This is how countries like Malaysia (where Malay Muslims dominate, but Hindus and Chinese have a reasonable share of political voice) and Singapore (where the Chinese are on top, and Malay Muslims and Hindus play subordinate roles) are run. The Savarkar vision of a Hindu Rashtra would thus have resembled something like a Malaysia or a Singapore, both successful countries today, but with an in-built acceptance of diversity that is not forced.

In India, the closest we have come to such an arrangement is in Kerala, where politics is religiously delineated, with strong Muslim and Christian parties pushing their agendas. What is missing is Hindu domination at the top, as Hindus are represented by weak caste-based parties (the Nairs and Ezhavas have their own parties). In short, Kerala is the opposite of what a Savarkar would have wanted, by allowing the minorities to play up their identities, but not Hindus. In Kerala, the Hindu part of the United Democratic Front is not shown to be representing overall Hindu interests but only that of their social group, while the Muslim and Christian parties, represented by the Indian Union Muslim League and various factions of the Kerala Congress, are clearly defined sectarian groups.

The problem is Congress secularism, as Ambedkar himself pointed out in his tract on Pakistan. Ideally, the Congress should have been a Hindu party at the top of a coalition of other religious parties, but it has turned out to represent nobody in the end. Is it any surprise that for two successive elections it has been reduced to the size of a regional party?

Coming back to the idea of a Hindu Rashtra, Ambedkar accepted the Renan, Westphalian sense of nationhood, ignoring the more nebulous—but more appropriate—Indian notion of nationhood that is civilizational in nature. Thus, any past or future idea of Hindu Rashtra must emerge from this sense of a sacred geography, which is what Savarkar was beginning to outline in his work *Hindutva*. The work of defining a Hindu Rashtra is still incomplete, and one hopes we will be able to get a clearer picture of not only what it is but also what it should be as we proceed with the remaining chapters in this book.

3

SAVARKAR GOT IT MORE OR LESS RIGHT

The term 'Hindu Rashtra' defies easy definition for a simple reason: it flows from the difficulty in defining Hinduism itself. In *Riddles in Hinduism*, which contains the core of Ambedkar's trenchant critique of Hinduism's contradictions and alleged absurdities, he dismissed Hinduism as 'a congeries of creeds and doctrines....' which 'shelters within its portals monotheists, polytheists and pantheists...'[1]

For Ambedkar, a Parsi, a Christian or a Muslim would know what his religion stands for and what he believes in, but a Hindu would be flummoxed when asked what makes him a Hindu.

The same idea, this time with a positive spin, was put forth by Gandhi, who said that Hinduism was not an exclusivist idea.

> Hinduism is not an exclusive religion. In it there is room for the worship of all the prophets in the world. It is not a missionary religion in the ordinary sense of the term.

> It has no doubt absorbed many tribes in its fold, but this absorption has been of an evolutionary, imperceptible character. Hinduism tells every one to worship God according to his own faith or Dharma and so it lives at peace with all the religions.[2]

This is not very different from what Swami Vivekananda said in his paper on Hinduism presented to the World Parliament of Religions in 1893: 'From the high spiritual flights of the Vedanta philosophy, of which the latest discoveries of science seem like echoes, to the low ideas of idolatry with its multifarious mythology, the agnosticism of the Buddhists, and the atheism of the Jains, each and all have a place in the Hindu's religion.'[3]

In short, Hinduism lives with many contradictions in its essential pluralism.

Others have found cultural, geographical and racial features in Hinduism to claim coherence for a national identity, which can be lumped under the rubric of Hindu Rashtra, and whose diverse peoples can be called Hindus.

For Sarvepalli Radhakrishnan, a scholar on Hinduism and second president of independent India, Hinduism was a 'way of life'. In *The Hindu View of Life*, he said: 'The differences among the sects of the Hindus are more or less on the surface and the Hindus as such remain a distinct cultural unit with a common history, a common literature, and a common civilisation.'[4]

Madhav Sadashiv Golwalkar, the charismatic second sarsanghchalak (head) of the RSS, saw Hindus as constituting a 'national race' in India,[5] while Savarkar held that all who regard the land 'from the Indus (Sindhu) to the Seas, as his fatherland (Pitrubhu) and Holy Land (Punyabhu) is a Hindu'.[6]

A Hindu, according to Savarkar, is thus one who 'addresses this land, this Sindhusthan, as his holy land (Punyabhu), as the land of his prophets and seers, of his godmen and gurus, the land of piety and pilgrimage'.[7] And the essentials of his idea of Hindutva were thus a common nation (rashtra), a common race (jati) and a common civilization (sanskriti). In theory, this implies that Muslims or Christians without extraterritorial religious loyalties would also fit this definition.

Yet, others saw nationalism as embedded in the Hindu idea of a sacred geography, a theme that appears repeatedly from the Rig Veda to the Atharva Veda, and which continues even today in the popular practice of going on pilgrimage, or *teerth yatras*.

In the Abrahamic tradition, while there are many pilgrimage spots, religion can be geography-neutral. In the Hindu case, all of its holy places are in India—or, Akhand Bharat, which is pre-Partition India.

In his book *Nationalism in Hindu Culture,* written more than a century ago, historian and scholar Radhakumud Mookerji noted:

> The institution of the pilgrimage is one of the distinguishing characteristics of ancient Hindu civilisation. In no other country of the world do we find such an elaborate network of shrines and sacred places as has been spread over this vast mother-country of ours by the religious enthusiasm of the people which has sought to adore the country in that particular manner. Indeed, if we carefully examine this peculiar institution that has made its influence felt throughout the country in all its parts and in all the ages of its history, we shall be bound to conclude that it is but one of the modes in which the patriotism of the Hindu has chosen to express itself.[8]

In short, Hindu Rashtra is a lot more about our sense of a sacred geography than theocracy.

The same idea found resonance in Eck's book, *India: A Sacred Geography*, where she notes that India is a 'land linked not by the power of kings and governments, but by the footsteps of pilgrims'.[9]

She adds:

> It is indisputable that an Indian imaginative landscape has been constructed in Hindu mythic and ritual contexts, most significantly in the practice of pilgrimage. The vast body of Hindu mythic and epic literature is not simply literature of devotional interest to the Hindu and of scholarly interest to the structuralist, comparativist, or psychoanalytically-minded interpreter. Hindu mythology is profusely linked to India's geography—its mountains, rivers, forests, shores, villages, and cities. It 'takes place', so to speak, in thousands of shrines and in the culturally created mental map of Bharata.[10]

This sense of a Hindu Rashtra situated in its own geography takes the form of viewing India, that is Bharat, as motherland. This was epitomized best in Bankim Chandra Chattopadhyay's 'Vande Mataram' (meaning, Mother, I bow to thee), the national song that, for many Hindus, has emotional parity with the national anthem, 'Jana Gana Mana'. Mother India is represented as a Goddess astride a lion.

The same thought process continues in the RSS's daily prayer at its shakhas, which begins with the words, *Namaste sada vatsale matrubhoomi* (I bow to thee forever, my motherland). The RSS is widely claimed to be a Hindu/ Hindutva organization, but in terms of its actual practice, it is not an organization that believes too much in Hindu rituals, rites and religious activities per se. Its key festivals are Varsh Pratipada, the most widely accepted Hindu New Year Day (in mid-April), Hindu Samrajya Din (Shivaji's coronation day), Guru Poojan, Raksha Bandhan, Vijayadashami and Makar Sankranti. It does not celebrate the more popular Hindu festivals of Holi and Diwali. The RSS celebrates 15 August as Akhand Bharat Din, not our conventional Independence Day.[11]

If one were to parse through all these ideas of what various writers and intellectuals thought of Hinduism and what might be construed as the key elements of a future Hindu Rashtra, three things become clear: one, a Hindu Rashtra would not be a mirror image of Pakistan in terms of establishing a theocratic state; two, its key definitions include an exclusive geographical loyalty to the sense of India as it has evolved through five millennia and as it has been imagined through its sacred literature; and three, a Hindu state may be defined by what it may not allow, and not what it may prescribe as mandated religious practices for its citizens.

Even in the Savarkarite rendering of a unified Hindu nation, there is space for Muslims and minorities—but without special privileges.

In one of his speeches as president of the Hindu Mahasabha, Savarkar said:

> When once the Hindu Maha Sabha not only accepts but maintains the principles of 'one-man-one-vote' [...] fundamental rights and obligations to be shared by all citizens alike irrespective of any distinction of Race or Religion [...] any further mention of minority rights is on the principle not only unnecessary but self-contradictory. Because it again introduces a

> consciousness of majority and minority on communal basis. But as practical politics requires it, and as the Hindu Sanghatanists want to relieve our non-Hindu countrymen of even a ghost of suspicion, *we are prepared to emphasise that the legitimate rights of minorities with regard to their Religion, Culture and Language will be expressly guaranteed* [emphasis added]—on one condition only—that the equal rights of the majority also must not in any case be encroached upon or abrogated. Every minority may have separate schools to train up their children in their own tongue, their own religious or cultural institutions and can receive government help also for these—but always in proportion to the taxes they pay into the common exchequer. The same principle must of course hold good in case of the majority too.
>
> Over and above this, in case the constitution is not based on joint electorates and on the unalloyed national principle of one-man-one-vote, but is based on the communal basis then *those minorities who wish to have separate electorate or reserved seats will be allowed to have them* [emphasis added]—but always in proportion to their population and provided that it does not deprive the majority also of an equal right in proportion of its population too.[12]

Remember, this was written well before it was clear that Pakistan would be created, and the proposals were made for an undivided India with a 'Hindu' majority and a large Muslim minority. Savarkar advocated proportionate representation for Muslims, which means their legislative powers would be very strong assuming Hindu MPs were not united in what they wanted. The only caveat is that the Constitution would not allow special rights to minorities (as under Articles 25 to 30 of the Indian constitution), while perversely denying the same to Hindus, as is the case now.

Savarkar's views would thus indicate that a Hindu Rashtra would be Hindu only in terms of its political dominance, but not theocratically so. And Muslims would not be submerged under it. But neither would Hindus be allowed to get submerged by increasing Muslim demography and other forms of population boost.

Savarkar said:

> The Moslem minority in India will have the right to be treated as equal citizens, enjoying equal protection and civic rights in proportion to their population. The Hindu majority will not encroach on the legitimate rights of any non-Hindu minority. But in no case can the Hindu majority resign its right which as a majority it is entitled to exercise under any democratic and legitimate constitution. *The Moslem minority in particular has not obliged the Hindus by remaining in minority and therefore, they must remain satisfied with the status they occupy and with the legitimate share of civic and political rights that is their proportionate due* [emphasis added]. It would be simply preposterous to endow the Moslem minority with the right of exercising a practical veto on the legitimate rights and privileges of the majority and call it a 'Swarajya.' The Hindus do not want a change of masters, are not going to struggle and fight and die only to replace an Edward by an Aurangzeb simply because the latter happens to be born within Indian borders, but they want henceforth to be masters themselves in their own house, in their own land.[13]

In a Hindu Rashtra, the principle of geography-based loyalty would imply that there would be laws to prevent inflows of foreign money for religious conversions, or border controls to prevent illegal migration from neighbouring countries. On the other hand, Hindus, Sikhs, Jains and Indic-origin Buddhists living outside India might be given the right to emigrate back to India if they so choose—something the Jewish state of Israel guarantees to Jews anywhere.

The last element of Hindu Rashtra could conceivably be the Upanishadic principle of *neti-neti*: neither this, nor that. Expounded in the Brihadaranyaka Upanishad by Sage Yagnavalkya, 'neti-neti' implies that the greatest truth can only be understood or experienced, not described in words. Hence, not this, nor that. Like the idea of atman, the ideas of a Hindu Rashtra may be defined not by what it should be, but what it should not be. And that implies that it cannot, should not, be theocratic in nature.

Given the essential plurality of Hinduism, where no one book, one prophet or one set of fundamentals is accepted by all, a Hindu Rashtra constitution may not tell citizens what to do, but what not to do.

It could, for example, forbid certain activities like active conversions even while preserving the individual's right to follow and practise any religion of his choice. True conversion is about adopting a better practice from another, not abandonment of one's own truths.

There would be no denial of other people's approaches to God and truth, only discouragement of Abrahamic ideas of decrying 'false gods' or designating non-believers as kafirs, among others. In the Rig Veda, where many tribes fought among themselves, the gods of the defeated peoples were never disgraced. They were always accepted.

A Hindu Rashtra would not stand in the way of a Muslim doing the haj or practising his religion but would draw the line at Indian Muslims asking their *ummah* to work against Hindu or Indian interests. Appeals to foreign powers to interfere in India's politics or laws would be explicitly forbidden. In April 2020, the then Delhi Minority Commission chief, Zafarul Islam Khan, loudly thanked Kuwait for standing by Indian Muslims, who, he claimed, were specially targeted during the Covid-19 lockdown. He claimed that Indian Muslims had so far not complained to the Arab world about their alleged persecution in India, but the day they are 'pushed to do that, bigots will face an avalanche'.[14] This appeal to outside powers to intervene in India's affairs happened again when Muslim nations unitedly spoke against a BJP spokesperson's references to the Prophet in a TV debate, discussed in an earlier chapter. It also happened earlier when a few Indian Muslims and Christians appealed to the US government to deny Narendra Modi a visa to visit that country after the post-Godhra riots of 2002.[15]

What Zafarul actually ended up doing was build a case for Hindu Rashtra in uncommitted Hindu minds by emphasizing precisely what Hindus fear: extraterritorial loyalties among its minorities.

One can surmise that the idea of a Hindu Rashtra is opposed not necessarily because of the actual threat it poses to minorities but because of one particularly stark statement made by Madhav Sadashiv 'Guru' Golwalkar in *We or Our Nationhood Defined*, where he made an unambiguous statement relegating Muslims to second-class citizenship.

He emphasized:

> The non-Hindu peoples of Hindustan must either adopt the Hindu culture and language, must learn to respect

> and hold in reverence Hindu religion, must entertain no ideas but those of the glorification of the Hindu race and culture [...] in a word, they must cease to be foreigners, or they may stay in the country wholly subordinated to the Hindu nation, claiming nothing, deserving no privileges, far less any preferential treatment, not even citizen rights.[16]

This is a statement that embarrasses even his own organization today, and in a nationally reported speech held in September 2018, RSS Chief Mohan Bhagwat said that the Sangh does not subscribe to this view. Bhagwat said: 'We have published a book titled "Vision and Mission: Guruji", which contain his eternal thoughts. We have removed all those thoughts that may have emerged in certain circumstances and included those that are eternal.'[17]

The critics who keep slamming Golwalkar forget one simple thing: what he enunciated in *Nationhood* is exactly what Islam prescribes for conquered peoples, or *dhimmies*, who are given limited rights and live as second-class citizens in Muslim-majority societies. No one who criticizes Golwalkar has even mentioned the idea of how dhimmies are treated in Islam. The RSS has recanted from Golwalkar's extreme position; Islamists have not.

This chapter, the bulk of which *Swarajya* published on 30 June 2020,[18] should make it clear that whatever else it may be, Hindu Rashtra is not about replicating a Hindu version of Islam in India.

4

OUR CONSTITUTION WRITTEN IN THE WRONG LANGUAGE

The case for a dharmic nation or Hindu Rashtra—even if one is not satisfied with the minimalist approach suggested in an earlier chapter—rests on whether or not it satisfies three criteria.

One, whether one accepts the idea of a civilizational state rooted in one's own inherited sense of societal self and values; two, whether this definition brings positive benefits for all stakeholders, including those who do not subscribe to the idea; and three, whether the current constitutional document, with some important modifications, can be good enough to support the idea without compromising its core values.

The world has broadly three kinds of states in existence: there are Westphalian nation-states, where race, religion and culture often combine to define a people resident in a specific, defensible geography. This is an idea that developed in the specific context of Europe's history and geography, and later spread to wherever Eurocentric cultures dominated.

The Westphalian idea of the nation-state originated in the seventeenth century, when scores of small and large states, principalities and kingdoms spent 30 years fighting in a brutal, free-for-all war with no decisive result.

History Today describes it thus:

> The war or series of connected wars began in 1618, when the Austrian Habsburgs tried to impose Roman Catholicism on their Protestant subjects in Bohemia. It pitted Protestant against Catholic, the Holy Roman Empire against France, the German princes and princelings against the emperor and each other, and France against the Habsburgs of Spain. The Swedes, the Danes, the Poles, the Russians, the Dutch and the Swiss were all dragged in or dived in. Commercial interests and rivalries played a part, as did religion and power politics.[1]

The war ended only when many of the warring states got tired of the endless conflict and saw the futility of continuing it. But it took four years (1644–48) of fractious negotiations to arrive at the final treaty—involving discussions and wrangling by over 194 states and their 179 plenipotentiaries—signed in Westphalia, a small town in north-western Germany. The treaty defined the rights and roles of the nation-state, where each state was sovereign in its own territory.

Outside Europe, there are nation-states based largely on ideas of race and ethnic monocultures (such as China, Japan and Korea, among others). These can also be called civilizational states, especially if their identities go back hundreds, if not thousands, of years.

Then there are nations defined largely by religious identity (such as Saudi Arabia, Pakistan and much of the Muslim world, where geography does not matter).

Israel can be considered a state based on a mix of religious and civilizational identity. And then there are modern 'secular' states which claim identities purely on the basis of a synthetic constitution (the US and much of modern Europe), though one can argue that their values are a kind of secularized Christianity.

India, according to a Left-liberal consensus, and most western historians, is a 'secular' state, whose nationhood is defined purely by a mix-and-match Constitution drawn from multiple other constitutions extant at the time it was drafted. India, according to this view, is a hotchpotch of various races, religious practices and linguistic diversities, with no prior sense of a common civilizational identity. Some Left-liberals also see India as a 'state-nation', a collection of states illogically grouped together into one 'nation'.

In one paper, Alfred Stepan, Juan K. Linz and Yogendra Yadav, the authors, ask:

> One of the most urgent conceptual, normative, and political tasks of our day is to think anew about how polities that aspire to be democracies can accommodate great sociocultural and even multinational diversity within one state. Must every state be a nation and every nation a state? Or should we look instead to the example of countries such as India, where one state holds together a congeries of 'national' groups and cultures in a single and wisely conceived federal republic?[2]

However, the answer to the question may not be the 'state-nation', for, even the sub-federal states of India are a 'congeries' of castes and communities, regional and sub-regional linguistic groups, and forest tribes and urban dwellers. The answer to the nation-state may thus lie in a loose idea called 'civilizational state'—a state defined by its people from the ground up, and not top-down by rulers.

As discussed in an earlier chapter, Radhakumud Mookerji noted more than a century ago that the Hindu national identity manifested itself in a common sense of a shared sacred geography and pilgrimage centres. More recently, J. Sai Deepak, an articulate lawyer who practises in the Delhi High Court and the Supreme Court, has written a series of articles on the idea of the civilizational state. His book, *India, That Is Bharat: Coloniality, Civilisation, Constitution*, published in 2021 and the first in a trilogy, has been a runaway hit, running into several impressions.

According to him, the western scholar's rejection of any idea of a nation outside the principle established by the Treaty of Westphalia has been largely accepted by post-colonial Indian scholars (usually from the Left), who see India as a state-nation, a collection of diverse nationalities welded together by their pre-1947 colonial masters.

In a series of articles published by *The Daily Guardian*, Sai Deepak writes:

> A closer reading of the history of the Constitution, its backdrop which includes the history of integration of states, may even reveal that the original intent of the framers of the document was to anchor it firmly in fertile and rich civilisational ground. After all, since Article 1 of the Constitution starts with 'India, that is Bharat,' it can be presumed within the bounds of reasonableness that the framers of the Constitution saw, India, i.e. Bharat, as the modern successor state to its civilisational ancient, making India a civilisational state. Such a reading of the Constitution is bound to have direct and indirect implications for several constitutional values and the treatment they have received thus far in political, social,

> cultural, academic and, of course, legal discourse. The Constitution's approach to every issue which grabs the attention of the nation, from religion to caste, morality to education, gender to sexuality, citizenship to migration, development to environment, history to national security, free speech to censorship, truth to reconciliation, politics to governance, and everything else in between, will need to be revisited in the light of the new or reclaimed civilisational paradigm.[3]

Subramanian Swamy points out in *The Ideology of India's Modern Right* that the original copy of the Constitution document had 22 illustrations to record India's 5,000-year-old cultural history—from epic heroes like Rama and Krishna to Hanuman, Buddha and Mahavira, and further to Akbar, Shivaji, Guru Gobind Singh and Rani Laxmibai.[4]

The only illustration that sticks out like a sore thumb is that of Tipu Sultan, whose bigotry is only now being recognized by many modern Hindus, but not 'secular' intellectuals. But he probably got into the original document by virtue of his resistance to British supremacy—an aspect of him which we need not ignore.

You can call it Bharat, or Hindu Rashtra, but we are talking of the same civilizational state that even our Constitution's creators subtly underscored. India, that is Bharat can, or should, be called a Hindu Rashtra, which, by definition, is a dharmic nation once you expand the idea beyond Hinduism to the other three major religions that were birthed here.

Here, Hindu does not mean the Hindu religion, but the Indic civilization, and a Hindu Rashtra that does not—in fact, cannot—discriminate against those who do not subscribe to this view. The need for defining a Hindu Rashtra today comes from some aspects of the Constitution that need amplification and reinterpretation.

Consider the Preamble, which reads thus:

> WE, THE PEOPLE OF INDIA, having solemnly resolved to constitute India into a SOVEREIGN SOCIALIST SECULAR DEMOCRATIC REPUBLIC and to secure to all its citizens:
>
> JUSTICE, social, economic and political; LIBERTY of thought, expression, belief, faith and worship;
>
> EQUALITY of status and of opportunity;
>
> and to promote among them all FRATERNITY assuring the dignity of the individual and the unity and integrity of the Nation;
>
> IN OUR CONSTITUENT ASSEMBLY this twenty-sixth day of November, 1949, do HEREBY ADOPT, ENACT AND GIVE TO OURSELVES THIS CONSTITUTION.

There is absolutely nothing wrong with this formulation of the Preamble, even if one were to exclude extraneous words such as 'socialist' and 'secular', which were incorporated in the mid-1970s, when Mrs Gandhi rewrote parts of the Constitution after sending many opposition leaders to jail. The insertions were her political response to the need to legitimize her internal Emergency. Otherwise, who can oppose the ideas of social justice, equality, brotherhood, etc.? And yet, if one accepts the idea of Bharat, how is it that words and expressions unique to our civilizational identities find no space, when French Revolution terms like 'liberty', 'equality' and 'fraternity' do? Why are words like 'dharma' (upholding a cosmic order), 'ahimsa' (non-violence), *artha* (wealth), *nyaya* (justice), *satya* (truth), *moksha* (freedom from rebirth), *antyodaya* (serving the poorest man), *sampradaya* (broadly denomination), 'varna' and 'jati' missing?

The last two terms are important precisely because we have to correct the injustices built into the varna-jati system, but reducing both ideas to just one word called 'caste'—a Portuguese term—and a single meaning of hierarchical oppression surely is problematic.

Aspects of kinship and social capital are completely missing when we confuse varna and jati, and combine both to mean just caste-based discrimination and oppression. In the process, caste is now the route to retaining the super-structure of oppression—for state-sponsored benefits depend on it—and not a way to transcend those narrow identities in a civilizational state called Bharat.

Can you end social oppression and inequities without even defining clearly this most important of Indic institutions that has survived well past its sell-by date?

It can be argued that words like 'dharma' have multiple meanings, but that charge can be levelled against words like 'equality' or 'justice' too. The word 'equality' can be interpreted in many ways, for one man's idea of it can be different from another's.

What kind of equality can we assure in an unequal world? Equality of opportunity or outcomes? We can choose the former, as the Preamble makes clear, but can human definitions truly clarify equality of opportunity in all its nuances?

We can define equality of opportunity relatively easily in a hobby like golf, where the better the player you are, the lower your handicap, which means you need to get the job done with fewer strokes than amateurs, or those with lower skills. But in life, can we really build a system to inflict handicaps on the better off that truly equalize opportunities for all?

And what role should merit play in this obsession with equality? And what if, even with handicaps (which, after all, will be decided by flawed humans using flawed mental models), outcomes are still skewed in favour of some? *Greater* equality, howsoever defined, may be a worthwhile goal in theory, but equality is always going to be an impossible ideal to achieve.

And what of justice? What do we mean by it? Isn't it often the case that justice can be acknowledged when it is seen to be done or delivered in a specific case, but cannot necessarily be defined too precisely for every context?

Sudhir Kakar, India's best-known psychoanalyst and author, raises some of these questions in an article he wrote for *The Times of India* in July 2019, pointing out that traditional Indian values of inclusiveness and sympathy are missing from today's political discourse.

> One feels that the traditional Indian civilisational emphasis on sympathy, love in its most elevated form, as indispensable to social cohesion and solidarity, is being eclipsed by other values, such as justice, the righting of wrongs. We are all familiar with the famous slogan of the French revolution, now a universal aspiration: Liberty, Equality, Fraternity. It is interesting to note that fraternity, brotherhood, occupies the last place in this short list and, indeed, has become completely muted if not sidelined in contemporary discourse.[5]

Ambedkar notes that even religious ideologies that specifically call for justice and brotherhood—Islam, for instance—fall far short of it in reality. He wrote in his pre-Independence tract on Pakistan:

> Hinduism is said to divide people and in contrast Islam is said to bind people together. This is only a half-truth. For Islam divides as inexorably as it binds. Islam is a close[d] corporation and the distinction that it makes between Muslims and non-Muslims is a very real, very positive and very alienating distinction. The brotherhood of Islam is not the universal brotherhood of man. It is brotherhood of Muslims for Muslims only. There is a fraternity, but its benefit is confined to those within that corporation. For those who are outside the corporation, there is nothing but contempt and enmity.[6]

But even within this 'closed corporation' of Islamic brotherhood, Ambedkar pointed out that caste distinctions and social evils remained strong. He concluded that 'Muslim society is even more full of social evils than Hindu society is'.[7]

The net effect is that justice is more about the aggregation of power in the hands of those claiming to deliver justice than really about ensuring a true brotherhood or sisterhood of equals.

Kakar points out that social justice is linked to power equations.

> Social movements in [the] service of justice for the weak and the oppressed are rapidly picking up pace in our country, shaking traditional hierarchies and power structures. This is a welcome development. Some of these movements, however, seem to operate on the basis of only one ethic, justice, which is related to the issue of power, of correcting skewed and unfair power relations, a highlighting of equality in the three aspirations of the French revolutionary slogan. In an almost sacralised ethic of justice, what matters is the

> outcome, not the path and there are eloquent voices that have defended violence in service of justice. In such cases, should the ethic of sympathy, compassion in this context, not temper the quest for justice?[8]

The point is that no matter what ideal of civilization you choose to extol—whether the French Revolution ones or the ones valued in a dharmic context like India's—actual implementation will always fall short. However, this gap is likely to be less serious if the ideals are those that are already in-built into a society. To be more precise, the ideals must resonate in the language the people understand instinctively.

One problem with the Indian constitution is that it was entirely conceived and written in a foreign language, English, which means its interpretation will also be alien to our culture even if our courts are Indian. When your law is written in a language different from your own myriad ways of expression, it becomes difficult to embed it as a value in your people. Thus, freedom of religion and secularism—ideas typical to the western context, where state and church agreed to a separation of powers against the backdrop of their own historical experiences—make little sense in a country that saw no need for this artificial separation.

The only English word that truly comes close to describing an Indic reality on inclusiveness is pluralism, not secularism. A civilization that preaches *Ekam Sat, Viprah Bahuda Vadanti* (There is one truth, the wise speak of it in many ways), is plural by nature. It does not require a constitution to mandate this. And what sense does separation of church and state make in a country with a large Muslim population, whose very history involves merging religious, social and political identities? The Prophet of Islam was a religious leader, political head and military commander all rolled into one.

As for Hindus, they are comfortable with multiple identities, and the formal separation of state and religion makes sense only in a limited way, where the state does not discriminate against one religion or the other. That, unfortunately, is not the case with the state and Hinduism, as we shall see later.

It is equally interesting that in the initial phase of Independence, essentially Indic—Vedic, Upanishadic and Puranic—terms like *Satyameva Jayate* (the national motto), *Dharmo Rakshati Rakshitah* (ideal of the Research and Analysis Wing), *Yato Dharmastato Jayah* (Supreme Court's baseline), *Bahujan Hitaya, Bahujan Sukhaya* (All India Radio), *Satyam Shivam Sundaram* (Doordarshan), *Seva Asmakam Dharmah* (Indian Army) and *Yogakshemam Vahamyaham* (LIC) were not seen as a Hindu imposition on the general population. The cultural rootedness indicated by the association of these terms with state institutions is now being challenged by Left-liberals in the name of political correctness.

Verses from the Upanishads, Panchatantra and the Mahabharata adorn Parliament's halls, as Swamy points out in *The Ideology of India's Modern Right*. Today, in a complete perversion of this civilizational heritage, even yoga and the mere rerun of the hugely popular *Ramayana* and *Mahabharata* serials on Doordarshan are seen as an antithesis of secularism, an imposition by Hindutva ideologues.

The reduction of Indic terms to English often results in a form of discrimination against those who claim this civilization and religious heritage. Thus, the use of the word 'denomination' in Article 26, which is translated as 'sampradaya' in the Hindi version of the Constitution, ensures that some Hindu sub-identities do not get the promised protections, including the right to run temples and maintain age-old religious rites and practices.

The five-judge bench judgment in the Sabarimala case, which delegitimized the practice of excluding women in the reproductive age from entering the shrine in a 4:1 September 2018 verdict, is an example of a perversion facilitated by the language in which the Constitution was written in.

While a new constitutional bench may still overturn this verdict, the interpretation of the word 'denomination' will remain problematic. When Indian jurisprudence is determined by terms that hold meaning only in a Eurocentric or Christian context, we surely have lost something in translation.

Article 26 guarantees:

> Freedom to manage religious affairs, subject to public order, morality and health. 'Every religious denomination or any section thereof shall have the right; (a) *to establish and maintain institutions for religious and charitable purposes;* (b) *to manage its own affairs in matters of religion;* (c) *to own and acquire movable and immovable property; and* (d) *to administer such property in accordance with law.*

The Hindi version of Article 26 runs thus:

लोक व्यवस्था, सदाचार और स्वास्थ्य के अधीन रहते हुए, प्रत्येक धार्मिक संप्रदाय या उसके किसी अनुभाग को–

(क) धार्मिक और पूर्त प्रयोजनों के लिए संस्थाओं की स्थापना और पोषण का,

(ख) अपने धर्म विषयक कार्यों का प्रबंध करने का,

(ग) जंगम और स्थावर संपत्ति के अर्जन और स्वामित्व का, और

(घ) ऐसी संपत्ति का विधि के अनुसार प्रशासन करने का, अधिकार होगा।

> *Lok vyavastha, sadachar aur swastya ke adheen rehte hue, pratyek dharmic sampradaya ya uske kisi anubhag ko*
> *(ka) dharmic aur poorth prayojanon ke liye sansthaon ki sthapana aur poshan ka,*
> *(kha) apne dharm vishyak karyon ka prabandh karne ka,*
> *(ga) jangam aur sthawar sampatti ke arjan aur swamithwa ka, aur*
> *(gha) aisi sampatti ka vidhi ke anusar prashasan karne ka adhikar hoga.*

The obvious meaning of the phrase *pratyek dharmic sampradaya ya uske kisi anubhag* should make every religious group or subgroup eligible to protections under Article 26, and yet the majority judgment effectively held that Swami Ayyappa's devotees were Hindu, and not a distinct sect or denomination within it, and hence not entitled to the protections guaranteed under Article 26.

Chief Justice Dipak Misra (retired) and Justices A.M. Khanwilkar (retired), D.Y. Chandrachud and Rohinton Fali Nariman (retired), who delivered the majority judgment, denied denominational status to Sabarimala's Swami Ayyappa devotees. Only the minority dissenting judgment of Justice Indu Malhotra accepted the devotees' claims of being a separate denomination in the judgment.[9]

In the Eurocentric context, the word 'denomination' goes well beyond the meaning assigned to it in the dictionary, which is 'a religious group that has slightly different beliefs from other groups that share the same religion' (*Cambridge English Dictionary*).

Believers in specific denominations often do not visit or offer prayers in churches managed by other denominations, and burials of the dead from one denomination may not be allowed in another.

This rigidity does not exist among Hindus, who use common crematoria for the dead, even though they may ordinarily follow their own sampradaya's traditions and rituals in various ceremonies, from birth to death. A Shaivite may worship at Vaishnavite temples and vice versa, or visit mutts of specific sampradayas with the same reverence he holds for his own favourite temples or religious organizations or gurus. And vice versa.

Articles 25 to 30 of the Indian constitution, originally meant to protect the religious, cultural and educational rights of all citizens, and especially minorities after a violent partition, have been interpreted by the Indian state to mean that the same rights can be denied to Hindu institutions on various pretexts, the most obvious one being 'mismanagement' of temples by traditional Hindu managers and priests. But 'secularists' will scream blue murder if a mosque or church were to be taken over for the same reasons.

Another way to deny equal rights to Hindus is by alleging 'untouchability', which Article 17 bans and prohibits. Justice Chandrachud (now Chief Justice of India), in his part of the Sabarimala judgment, directly drew a link between 'untouchability' and the exclusion of women in the reproductive age from entering the shrine. Once anyone uses the dreaded word 'untouchability' in any context, it is possible for the state or the judiciary to intervene in Hindu religious affairs, which they would not do with other religious institutions.[10]

The word 'secular', originally formulated in the European

context to separate the powers of temporal rulers from spiritual ones, i.e. separation of state and church, is meaningless in the Indian context, where plurality and the right to follow your own religious inclinations are embedded in the civilizational ethos. However, the Constitution's provision to prevent discrimination on the basis of caste has been repeatedly used to ensure that it is mostly Hindu institutions that will be interfered with. To top it all, a straightforward violation of the norms of equal treatment and non-discrimination has resulted in the state positively discriminating in favour of the minorities.

Thus, we have minority ministries and minority commissions at central and state levels, which essentially offer favours to the minorities. The Right to Education Act specifically excludes—with a 93rd Constitutional Amendment—some unaided minority-run institutions from the obligation to educate the socially backward classes that majority-run institutions have to willy-nilly accept.

The case for tweaking the Constitution to enable the state to end this discrimination against the majority community, and to preserve and protect its ancient heritage, including by making laws to prevent aggressive religious conversion activities, thus stands strong.

Besides, the Indian civilizational state owes a responsibility to those who share this heritage, and may be persecuted elsewhere.

The Citizenship (Amendment) Act, 2019, which seeks to fast-track citizenship to Hindus and other minorities persecuted by three Muslim-majority states in the neighbourhood—Afghanistan, Bangladesh and Pakistan—is one step in this direction, but has run into legal and political wrangles, where its opponents allege that it goes against the

Constitution's basic norm of non-discrimination on the basis of religion.

To sum up, one can conclude three things: one, the English-based Indian constitution needs a few tweaks to make it compatible with what is the natural rhythm of Indic society. It is one thing to think in English and translate it in Sanskrit or Hindi equivalents, quite another to use the Indic word and then find equivalents in English. For example, religion can be translated as 'dharma', but 'dharma' is non-translatable into English without context. If the word had been used in the original English constitution, it would have carried more value with its nuances than now, when it is a word used to find an equivalent word to religion in Sanskrit. Dharma means several things, including the upholding of a broader cosmic order and a proper balance between two or more options, among others. Its meaning changes with the context. We have reduced the import of the word and its meanings by merely using it to translate an English word.

We are a civilization that sees no contradiction between the spiritual and the temporal, and secularism has no meaning for us. We might have had a different experience if our Constitution was first written in an Indian language, say, Hindi, and then translated into English, but that is now not likely. So, tweaks are needed to make the Constitution's provisions compatible with our civilizational ethos.

Two, amending the Constitution will not impact the rights of people who do not consider themselves Hindu because the protections of Articles 25 to 30 and the one on non-discrimination will remain even in a 'Hindu Rashtra' constitution that prioritizes the protection of Indic religious and cultural rights. And three, these changes are vital to prevent the Constitution from becoming a tool for

Hinduphobic law-making by giving its words Eurocentric and colonial meanings that are irrelevant to Bharat, that is India.

In future chapters, we will look more closely at some of the provisions of the Constitution that need change.

5

FREEDOM OF RELIGION—OR WHAT PASSES FOR IT

In July 2020, Turkey's Islamist president Recep Tayyip Erdoğan announced that the historic Hagia Sophia, the erstwhile power hub of the Byzantine Empire and the Greek Orthodox Church, would be converted as a mosque[1] and namaz (Friday prayers) offered from the 24th of the same month.

Built in the fourth century by Emperor Constantius, the church, which then had a wooden roof, was burnt down in the first decade of the fifth century in politically induced rioting. It was burnt down again a century later during the reign of Justinian I, who ruled from CE 527–65. The old church was demolished and rebuilt with renowned architects by Justinian, and it is this church that stands tall even today.

When the Ottoman Turks conquered Constantinople in 1453 and renamed it Istanbul, the church was converted to a mosque, even though the previous structure and mosaics remained. The new rulers, with Islam as their faith, renovated the church to look like a mosque, with original Christian themes being replaced with Islamic calligraphy. In the secular Turkey established by Mustafa Kemal Atatürk after the First

World War, the Hagia Sophia was converted into a museum in the 1930s. Now, with a Turkish High Court annulling the Atatürk decision, Hagia Sophia is back to being a mosque, with its former Christian mosaics being relegated to remain behind curtains or staying unlit during namaz.

The Pope has said he was 'very distressed'[2] with Erdoğan's decision, and the World Council of Churches had written to the latter expressing their 'grief and dismay'[3]. Erdoğan, who is trying to paint himself as the new leader of the Islamic world, has rubbished such protests, indirectly calling it Islamophobia. Aljazeera quotes him as saying, 'Those who do not take a step against Islamophobia in their own countries ... attack Turkey's will to use its sovereign rights.'[4]

The two points to note are these: the two main Abrahamic religions have a binary approach to religion. If one exists, the other must not. When Christianity rose to prominence, pagan places of worship were systematically demolished. It is worth noting that even in India, the Portuguese Christian Inquisition in Goa led to similar demolitions of temples and reprisals against Hindus who refused to convert, as documented in Anant Kakba Priolkar's *The Goa Inquisition: The Terrible Tribunal for the East.*[5] For Islam's depredations in India, you can do no better than to read Sita Ram Goel's monumental documentation of temple destruction in two volumes, *Hindu Temples: What Happened to Them*. More recently, mediaeval historian Meenakshi Jain has added to this literature of Islamic iconoclasm and destruction in *Flight of Deities and Rebirth of Temples: Episodes from Indian History.*[6]

In the Abrahamic tradition, it is either zero or one.

Second, the church and the mosque are symbols of political power and not just monuments to religiosity. This is why wherever these religions seek to expand, size and scale are all-important. In several Indian cities, you will see the Christian Cross tower over the skyline even in places with few church-goers. The idea is to herald the power of Christian belief.

Erdoğan's need to convert the Hagia Sophia into a mosque is linked to his ambition to lead the Islamic world. The Saudis have Mecca and Medina. Shia Iran, while continuing to see these two holy sites as central to their own version of Islam, has built the largest mosque in the world at Mashhad, which is Iran's main pilgrimage city. It houses the tomb and shrine of the eighth Shia Imam, Imam Reza.

By converting Hagia Sophia into a mosque, Erdoğan is creating his own Mecca to burnish his claims to leadership of the Muslim world, as was the case under the Ottoman Turks. He will be expecting Muslims from all over to head to Istanbul, giving it some of the power associated with Mecca, Medina and Al-Aqsa in Jerusalem.

In one line, both church and mosque are as much about projecting power as religiosity. When you project power, you get to set the terms of debate, discussion and even the meanings of common sense terms like 'freedom'.

In a global conversation defined more by existing power equations, cultural hegemony and hypocrisy, it is easy to rubbish the civilizational state of Hindu Rashtra as inimical to the idea of freedom of religion, free speech and fair treatment to all citizens. How much of free speech is hate speech when the limits of neither have been defined by common consensus? In the US, microblogging site Twitter hid a tweet of former US president, Donald Trump, for allegedly glorifying violence.[7] It flagged another tweet for violating its policies.[8] By that standard, holy books calling for the killing of infidels, too, should be hidden from public view.

Today, hate speech is not defined by normative definitions, but by the power elites, aka 'liberals'.

When it comes to freedom of religion, the question to ask is: whose freedom are we trying to protect? Are we talking about the rights of the individual to pursue any, all or parts of some religion that he likes, or the rights of multi-billion dollar evangelical corporations and conversion merchants who seek to sell religion like soap, by fair means or foul?

Everyone acknowledges that no freedom is absolute, and there can be reasonable restraints imposed by the state. If Article 19 of the Indian constitution prescribes limits to free speech and expression, then similar restraints on freedom of religion can hardly be considered inimical to the idea of religious freedom.

The free speech argument was tested in the US, and upheld by a narrow majority in the Supreme Court more than a decade ago. It generated much anger among the Democrats because it equalized the rights of unequals. The judgment revolved around a literal interpretation of the First Amendment to the US constitution which guarantees almost total freedom of speech and religion. The First Amendment reads: 'Congress shall make no law respecting an establishment of religion, or prohibiting the free exercise thereof; or abridging the freedom of speech, or of the press; or the right of the people peaceably to assemble, and to petition the government for a redress of grievances.'[9]

The US Supreme Court, through a 5:4 majority judgment delivered in 2010,[10] essentially held that corporations had the same political rights to free speech as individuals. In a case involving *Citizens United versus the Federal Election Commission*, the court held that restrictions on corporations and unions from spending money to back or oppose political candidates violated the First Amendment right to free speech.

Citizens United, a conservative NGO, had sought to air an anti-Hillary Clinton documentary just before the primaries in 2008—a political act barred by the Bipartisan Campaign Reform Act, 2002, which prohibits such campaign expenditures for a specific time before a primary or general election. The majority judgment was written by Judge Anthony Kennedy, and the minority one by Associate Judge John Paul Stevens, who pointed out that the court's ruling essentially rejected the 'common sense of the American people, who have recognized a need to prevent corporations from undermining self-government'.[11] The majority judgment overturned the bipartisan law, which prohibited corporations and unions from using their general funds for electioneering purposes, especially to elect or defeat candidates.

Barack Obama, who was president at the time of the Supreme Court judgment, blasted the verdict. He told the Congress in his State of the Union address that the court had 'reversed a century of law that I believe will open the floodgates for special interests—including foreign corporations—to spend without limit in our elections. I don't think American elections should be bankrolled by America's most powerful interests, or worse, by foreign entities. They should be decided by the American people. And I'd urge Democrats and Republicans to pass a bill that helps to correct some of these problems'.[12]

Clearly, the majority judgment is not the last word in the battle over free speech, but the logic of the much better argued minority judgment should apply to freedom of religion too: is it about the individual's right to follow a religion or religious practices of his choice, or the right of well-funded conversion outfits to induce people to shift religious loyalties in a game of numbers?

America is clearly split on this issue, but evangelical organizations believe that freedom of religion includes the right to deploy any and every method to convert people to worship 'the one true god' as opposed to the 'false gods' of other religions. This, at least, is what underlies the creation of the United States Commission on International Religious Freedom (USCIRF), which periodically rants against India and other non-Christian countries for curtailing religious freedoms, especially by (ineffectually) enforcing anti-conversion laws.

That the First Amendment specifically bars the state from interfering in matters of religion did not stop the Congress from adopting a bipartisan law to establish the USCIRF to police 'freedom of religion' in areas *outside* the US. In fact, the commission is barred from investigating the issue within the US, possibly to technically stay on the right side of the First Amendment. The USCIRF website makes it clear, and states that 'USCIRF monitors the universal right to freedom of religion or belief abroad—not in the United States—using international standards to do so, and makes policy recommendations to the President, Secretary of State, and Congress. USCIRF Commissioners are appointed by the President and Congressional leaders of both political parties. While USCIRF is separate from the State Department, the Department's Ambassador-at-Large for International Religious Freedom is a non-voting ex officio Commissioner'.[13]

In short, Uncle Sam, despite separating state from religion, actually appoints members to the USCIRF, and one nominee of the state department is even a member—non-voting one though he or she may be. Reading between the lines, one cannot but point out the hypocrisy of the state not intervening in religion, and then mandating one of its own creations to do so in other countries.

Jakob De Roover, faculty member on Comparative Science of Cultures at Ghent University, emphasizes that the USCIRF is about enforcing a Protestant view of 'freedom of religion' on the world rather than real freedom of religion in its common sense meanings. In an article in *Firstpost*, he wrote:

> The USCIRF's annual reports reflect these deep-seated religious concerns of Protestant Christianity. Take its vehement rejection of anti-conversion legislation in India as a violation of religious freedom. This derives from the Christian belief that every individual should be free to turn towards the true God at all times and that this can be done only by converting from false to true religion. For the US commission, this freedom to follow one's own conscience always overrides other concerns—say, for instance, the worry often voiced in India that Christian missionary activity constitutes aggression upon the traditions, sensitivities, and harmony of a community.
>
> Why? Well, protecting individual religious freedom has to do with safeguarding the right of every person to follow the will of the true God, which supersedes any issue that is merely human, such as the peace or stability of some social group. Hence, the fact that missionary work involves abusing the Hindu traditions as 'false religion' or their *devas* and *devis* as 'false gods' is considered much less problematic than putting restrictions on conversion. The fact that converts often insult the traditions to which they previously belonged is irrelevant when compared to the individual's freedom of religion. The fact that family and community life are

> severely disrupted because of proselytisation is a trivial detail in the face of the eternal human choice between true and false religion, between God and the devil.[14]

Contrast this with the wording of the Universal Declaration of Human Rights, which includes the right to freedom of religion and conscience. The key Article 18 on religious freedom runs thus: 'Everyone has the right to freedom of thought, conscience and religion; this right includes freedom to change his religion or belief, and freedom, either alone or in community with others and in public or private, to manifest his religion or belief in teaching, practice, worship and observance.'[15]

The only marginally problematic word from a non-proselytizing Hindu perspective is 'teaching', which in the Indian constitution appears as the right to propagate a religion. Article 25 guarantees citizens the right to 'Freedom of conscience and free profession, practice and *propagation* of religion [emphasis added]', but it does not define the word 'propagation'. Some court judgments, however, have sought to do just that, but the discourse around conversion has not changed.

In *Rev. Stainislaus vs State of Madhya Pradesh & Others* (January 1977), the Supreme Court held that the word 'propagate' in Article 25 of the Indian constitution means the right to teach the tenets of one's religion but not the right to convert. The judgment, inter alia, said:

> What the Article grants is not the right to convert another person to one's own religion, but to transmit or spread one's religion by an exposition of its tenets. It has to be remembered that Article 25 (1) guarantees 'freedom of conscience' to every citizen, and not merely

> to the followers of one particular religion, and that, in turn, postulates that there is no fundamental right to convert another person to one's own religion because if a person purposely undertakes the conversion of another person to his religion, as distinguished from his effort to transmit or spread the tenets of his religion, that would impinge on the 'freedom of conscience' guaranteed to all the citizens of the country alike.[16]

Few people would have a problem with allowing anyone to practise their religion or talk about its tenets unless these violate an individual's personal human rights (like the practice of female genital mutilation, triple talaq in one sitting or practising untouchability in the name of upholding Hindu dharma). The issue really is about propagation and its limits. If one were to take the minority view in the Citizens United judgment in the US, which is about freedom of speech, rights are about real individuals, not artificial persons such as corporations or unions, or, for that matter, churches or mosques. The rights of the latter must always remain limited in democracies. Else money power will trump the human spirit. The one exception to this rule of the rights of natural persons versus organizations is the Hindu worship of deities, where legally and in religious practice, the deity is treated as a real person.

On the other hand, there is the even more important issue of retaining the world's diversities. Freedom to convert people from pagan and other religions to the world's main monotheisms cannot by any stretch of imagination be called an attempt to maintain diversity. Christian universalism and the determination to convert all people to believe in the 'one true god' destroyed Hellenism in the ancient world,[17] and African cultures in the modern world.[18]

Some writers like Kendi Borona believe that 'colonial Christianity is the biggest problem in Africa'.[19] The more evangelical the brand of Christianity, the more damaging it is to diversity and culture.[20]

However, despite some attempt at introspection, the fundamental problem with one-true-god religions is that they are inherently against diversity in matters of faith. They may be okay with integrating and 'digesting' or appropriating some of the good aspects of rival religions and cultures, but the bottom line still is 'my God is the only true God'.

It is interesting that the Rig Veda, the oldest scared text of the Sindhu–Saraswati civilization, talks of many tribal and other conflicts over territory and resources, but the redeeming feature is that the gods of the defeated tribes were seldom dishonoured. In fact, the very last verse of the Rig Veda, Hymn 191 in the tenth mandala, has this to say about seeking unity (verse translation by Ralph T.H. Griffith, English Indologist).

> Thou, mighty Agni, gatherest up all that is precious for thy friend.
> Bring us all treasures as thou art enkindled in libation's place
> Assemble, speak together: let your minds be all of one accord,
> As ancient Gods unanimous sit down to their appointed share.
> The place is common, common the assembly, common the mind, so be their thought united.
> A common purpose do I lay before you, and worship with your general oblation.

> One and the same be your resolve, and be your minds of one accord.
>
> United be the thoughts of all that all may happily agree.[21]

The emphasis here is the search for unity in diversity, and fundamental to this is the underlying idea that all gods are valid sources of spiritual and religious respect. So, if one were to expand on the core credo of Hindu Rashtra, it would be this simple one: that all gods are created equal, and there can be no discrimination against one or the other. A corollary would be that religions that have a binary approach to God (my God or the highway) will be allowed to practise and preach but not propagate this aspect of their doctrines with the idea of conversion.

Philosopher Karl Popper's paradox asked a simple question: can a tolerant society be tolerant of the intolerant? His answer is not that a tolerant society must silence the intolerant, but that it must have the power to do so. If not, the intolerant will destroy the tolerant. The only limit on the proselytizing religions in a Hindu Rashtra would be their ability to preach intolerance and supremacist ideas about the only true god and demonization of the rest, including agnostics and atheists. This was what the Calcutta Koran petition of the mid-1980s sought to invoke by pointing out that several passages in the holy book demanded violence against non-believers.[22] But as Muslim organizations went on the warpath, both the courts and the central and state governments quickly junked the petition and erased its existence by never talking about it.

The petition is important not for what it demanded—the withdrawal of the offending paragraphs in the Koran—but for what it confirmed about the Popper Paradox: the intolerant often tend to win such arguments. As an aside, one can point out that one cannot seek to edit or expunge sacred literature today; what we can however do is reinterpret them, or de-emphasize those aspects that are not in tune with current ethical requirements.

It is worth re-emphasizing that in India, various religious and ethical ideas have been established, contested and reformed all through history. No religion originating in India sought to deny the possibility of embracing other ideas, or even deny the very need for religion. Conversions were about imbibing ideas, not changing identities. Gandhi is one such example. He was greatly inspired by Jesus Christ's *Sermon on the Mount*, and made it his life's guiding principle even while always maintaining that he was a Sanatani Hindu. That's conversion through the power of an idea which does not result in a damaging schizophrenia about one's personal identity. Gandhi did not have to become George in order to draw inspiration from *Sermon on the Mount*.

So, if one were to ask how a future Hindu Rashtra would define freedom of religion, and what kind of restraints it may place on conversions, the answer would run something like this: religious freedom would be an individual right and not available to corporate bodies, even if they are non-profits. There could also be limitations or bans on inflows of foreign funds to such organizations.

It is worth noting that, in addition to the freedoms enshrined in the UN Declaration of Human Rights, there is a separate UN Declaration on the Rights of Indigenous Peoples adopted by the General Assembly on 13 September 2007, though it is not clear that Hindu traditions and rights are covered by this declaration.[23]

The first paragraphs of the declaration are worth quoting.

They affirm that 'indigenous peoples are equal to all other peoples' and recognize 'the right of all peoples to be different, to consider themselves different, and to be respected as such'. It also affirms that 'all peoples contribute to the diversity and richness of civilisations and cultures, which constitute the common heritage of humankind', and '*that all doctrines, policies and practices based on or advocating [the] superiority of peoples or individuals on the basis of national origin or racial, religious, ethnic or cultural differences are racist, scientifically false, legally invalid, morally condemnable and socially unjust*' [emphasis added].

It further reaffirms that 'indigenous peoples, in the exercise of their rights, should be free from discrimination of any kind' since they have 'suffered from *historic injustices as a result of, inter alia, their colonisation and dispossession of their lands, territories and resources, thus preventing them from exercising, in particular, their right to development in accordance with their own needs and interests* [emphasis added].'

The Abrahamic religions claim explicit superiority of their faith over the rest, and Indic faiths have been repressed periodically during Islamic and colonial rule. Even today, state control of temples prevents Hindus from exercising their right to development in accordance with their own needs and interests.

One could ask whether the various sects and sampradayas of Hinduism constitute 'indigenous peoples' and whether their rights have the same importance as those tribal and pagan faiths that are smaller and localized in size. But the declaration makes no reference to the size of any indigenous culture or its own internal diversity. This implies that all tribal, natural and animist faiths that developed in the Indian subcontinent, including those now calling themselves Hindu, have the right to be called indigenous. Hindu Rashtra should be about protecting the world's diversity and the rights of India's indigenous religions and people from Abrahamic standardization and homogenization through conversions.

6

DEFINING HINDUTVA

India's 'secular liberals' have gotten their knickers in a twist over the rise of 'Hindutva' ideology. They have a right to fear its rise, for it threatens their own ideological hegemony, but their arguments to debunk the idea are completely self-serving or even illogical.

In this chapter, we will discuss their arguments, especially the main one that Hindutva is not Hinduism. We shall also attempt to define Hindutva in a way that is not reductionist, which is what its critics would like to do. They would like the term to be associated only with mob lynching or hate speech. A third element of this chapter will be to establish a need for the Hindutva project, and its positive and potentially negative angles. Overall, I would like emphasize that, warts and all, Hindutva may be more beneficial than diverse and disunited Hinduism with no coherent structure beyond caste.

Congress MP Shashi Tharoor, who wrote not one but two books on Hinduism (*Why I Am a Hindu* and *The Hindu Way*), is one of those 'liberals' who hopes that Hinduism and Hindutva will be mortal enemies. I read his first book with great interest to understand how Tharoor discovered his 'Hindu-ness', but halfway through the book, you realize that he daubs saffron on his sunshades only to mark out Hindutva as a villain.[1] The whole point of the book is to explain what is *not* Hinduism. He thinks Hindutva is an assault on Hinduism.[2] On the contrary, 'secularism' is more likely to be an assault on Hinduism, as one has shown in an earlier chapter, and will explain again in some of the forthcoming chapters.

A simple way to debunk this misconception is this: when liberal Hinduism does not reduce religion to one particular set of beliefs—one book, one prophet, one Son of God or one set of fundamentals—to presume that one cannot be a votary of Hindutva while claiming Hindu-ness is a logical fallacy. An idea can be antithetical to another only if you define both, and these definitions cannot be arbitrary or reductionist. Like Hinduism, Hindutva comes in many shades. Savarkar's Hindutva was not about the religion, for sure, but it was about protecting Hinduism for those who want to practise it any which way they want.

Columnist, economist and journalist Swaminathan S. Anklesaria Aiyar fell into the same trap, and tried to differentiate Hinduism from Hindutva in an article in *The Times of India*.[3] Apparently riled by the abuse he got on Twitter for suggesting that the Ayodhya Ram Mandir is of no consequence to Hindus or Hinduism, he followed it up with another piece to make precisely this point. He wrote: 'The media has tom-tommed the bhoomi pujan of the Ram temple as a major event for all Hindus. Sorry, but it is an event for Hindutva, not Hinduism.'

In support of this argument, he trots out his mother's beliefs. She apparently spent the last two decades of her life as a *sanyasin* (ascetic) at the Sivananda Ashram in Rishikesh, which made her 'a devout Hindu'. Aiyar also tells us—she isn't there to confirm this claim—that she would have decried the destruction of the Babri Masjid as the handiwork of 'thugs', 'a disgrace to all that was good and great in Hinduism'.

Let us, for starters, ignore the hypocrisy of someone who thinks of himself as an atheist to extol the virtues of some parts of the faith he left behind as 'good and great'. It's the lion singing the praises of deer to cock a snook at other prey that may be faster on their feet.

Then, he talks about Savarkar's Hindutva, which was not about religion at all. Aiyar writes:

> Savarkar strongly opposed traditional Hindu beliefs and viewed Hindutva as a politico-cultural rather than religious project. He hated Muslims. In some speeches he called himself an atheist, though more correctly he rejected the old Sanatan Dharma and sought a major modernisation of Hinduism. He said there was nothing sacred about cows and advised Hindus to give up vegetarianism. Savarkar's biographer, Dhananjay Keer, points out that when his wife died, despite entreaties by his followers, he refused to allow any Hindu rituals. I wish the Hindutva trolls would highlight this.

Again, let us ignore Aiyar's put-down in referring to his critics as Hindutva 'trolls' (after all, can someone who believes in Hindutva be anything but a troll?), and focus on his illogic. If he can, half-approvingly, bracket himself and Savarkar as atheists, and define Hindutva as a 'politico-cultural rather than religious project', why should he assume that there is no intersection between the two, the religious and the politico-cultural? Can a temple-going Hindu not believe in the Hindutva project, too? If he can believe that a Hindu can be secular, surely he should be able to conceive of a Hindu who is politically keen to seek a broader identity under the label of Hindutva?

If Hinduism is a broad enough tent to house all kinds of beliefs (and disbeliefs) and ideological inclinations, why should it be seen as inimical to Hindutva, which may be at least a new dimension of Hindu-ness? It may not be shared by all Hindus, but that does not make it any less Hindu in character.

It is as pointless to claim that Hindutva is not Hinduism as it is to suggest that modern Christianity has nothing to do with Jesus. While Jesus might have been the inspiration behind the creation of various churches soon after his crucifixion, Christ himself cannot be said to have literally founded any of his churches.[4] Latter-day versions of Christianity, from Anglo-Saxon Protestantism to Latin American liberation theologists, can hardly claim to be Christians when Jesus offered no clarifications on who can call himself (or herself) his follower.

The same can be said of Islam, Sikhism or Buddhism. The Prophet could not have imagined that his politico-religious ideology would be explained by his followers through his biography, the Hadith and the Sunnah, and that entirely different theologies—Shi-ism, Bahai-ism and Ahmadiyya-ism—would blaze new trails of their own. Guru Gobind Singh's Sikhism is different from Guru Nanak's, and the Buddha never even intended to establish a new religion—only a different way of dealing with the world, based on enlightenment and acceptance of suffering. But the bust of Buddha is now the world's most replicated icon after that of Jesus Christ on the Cross and various Hindu gods in different avatars and incarnations.

The question that arises is: why has it become necessary to demonize Hindutva? Why does it send shivers down the spines of 'secular liberals'?

The answer is Orientalism—the need to deconstruct a land and its peoples into a sum of the parts rather than the whole. The author of the book *Orientalism*, Edward W. Said, used the term to define the contemptuous western attitudes to things eastern, especially Islam.[5] This attitude now pervades western Indology, and its allies in India's 'Left-liberal' world.

This obviously makes it easier for expansionist and imperialist faiths, such as Christianity and Islam, to make inroads into Hinduism, which is precisely the result Hindutva would seek to deny them. Current attempts to deny Hindutva legitimacy have been preceded by wholesale attempts to even deny that there was anything called Hinduism before colonial scholars started dissecting the indigenous faiths and practices of the people they ruled over. In the Orientalist view, India became a political and social reality only after it was conquered, first by Muslim invaders and later by British colonialists.

This is obviously untrue, but the fear that writing the whole truth about India's past will somehow strengthen Hindus and Hindu nationalism runs deep among India's 'secular-liberal' intellectuals, such as Tharoor and Aiyar, and western Indologists and academicians in general. Take Harvard's professor of comparative religion and Indian studies, Diana L. Eck, who wrote *India: A Sacred Geography*. The author beautifully defines India as a 'land linked not by the power of kings and governments, but by the footsteps of pilgrims'.[6] This is pretty much what the late Radhakumud Mookerji said in his books, *The Fundamental Unity of India* and *Nationalism in Hindu Culture*. As we noted in an earlier chapter, Mookerji saw the unique Hindu institution of the theerth yatra as the invisible thread binding Hindus to one another despite living under different political dispensations.

And yet, in the very first chapter of her book, Eck frets over whether this cultural unity is going to feed Hindu nationalism. She writes: 'This is a book about India, the pilgrim's India. For a time, I was discouraged about the writing of it, fearing that somehow the image of a sacred geography enlivened by the presence of the gods and interlinked through the circulation of pilgrims would further feed the fervour of an exclusive new Hindu nationalism.'[7]

It is appalling that a scholar should be concerned that her truth will help someone she dislikes, instead of merely focussing on telling the story as she sees it. It is a westerner's attempt to sit in judgment on how Hindus should see themselves, or what they must do (or not do) to preserve their heritage and unity in the face of challenges.

Today's 'secular liberals' are thus playing the same role as sepoys of western imperialism—both the Indologist and academic writers—who want to limit what Hindutva or Hindu-ness should mean for Hindus.

This brings us to the basic question: what really is Hindutva? How is it different, or not different, from the word 'Hindu'?

Hindutva can be differentiated from the word 'Hindu' only in the sense that it is *not* merely about the practice of religious rites and rituals, or how any Hindu should interpret his faith or practices. You can go to temples, perform pujas, sing bhajans or eat sattvic foods as is your normal practice, and you can still call yourself a votary of Hindutva. You can be a Hindutva-vadi even if you do none of those things—as was the case with Savarkar, and even today's RSS, which believes in celebrating Guru Purnima and *rashtra bhakti* (patriotism) but seldom participates in popular Hindu festivals like Diwali or Holi. Many Sangh swayamsevaks do not even think of temple-going as an essential activity for a demonstration of their Hindu identity.

What we are getting at is this: Hindutva can be many things, but it is essentially an attempt to build a unifying identity—social, cultural and political—for all those who call themselves Hindus. It is an attempt to break out of the caste straitjacket, something that has always left Hindus vulnerable to proselytization and evisceration from within. (For the word 'caste', the meaning should be taken as the varna–jati construct, without conflating the two. The word 'caste' is being used for the sake of simplicity, and not to mix up varna and jati, which are two different things.)

Rajiv Malhotra, who is widely acknowledged as an intellectual Kshatriya battling to save Hinduism from being hijacked by Orientalists, western Indologists and their sepoys in India, sees Hindutva as some kind of 'political Hinduism[8].' Sankrant Sanu, one of the authors of *The English Medium Myth: Dismantling Barriers to India's Growth*, is a researcher, entrepreneur and book publisher who works out of Seattle and Gurgaon (now Gurugram). His definition of Hindutva is 'Hinduism that resists'.[9]

Walter K. Andersen, author of two of the most authoritative books on the RSS (his latest, *The RSS: A View to the Inside*, was coauthored with Shridhar D. Damle), explains the Hindutva dilemma thus: 'Hindutva's core value is the unity of Hindus. But Hindus' hierarchical caste system stands in the way of that.'[10]

What Andersen does not spell out, since he, too, thinks Hinduism may be inimical to Hindutva, is the obvious reality that Hindutva is the only logical way to reduce the impact of caste discrimination and hierarchy by unfolding a larger umbrella under which castes can forge a common identity.

In that sense, it is an attempt to create a broader cultural connect between Hindu groups, so that caste does not turn out to be a self-destructive form of diversity that makes Hinduism incapable of defending itself against its enemies and rivals.

At this stage, we need to digress into a discussion on monotheism and how it has been a necessary institution for the spread of imperialism and western universalism. We need to discuss this because monotheistic ideas are essential for religious and temporal forms of imperialism, and imperialism can only be countered through nationalism and some forms of cultural unity, which is what the Hindutva project is all about.

The link between monotheism and imperialism was first made by the father of western psychoanalysis, Sigmund Freud, in his book on *Moses and Monotheism*, written in 1939. In an earlier discussion on this topic in another publication (*DNA*), I had drawn on Freud's analysis to explain why empire-builders and imperialists needed monotheism to consolidate power.[11]

Freud wrote: 'Imperialism was reflected in religion as universality and monotheism,' adding, 'Religious intolerance, which was foreign to antiquity before this and long after, was inevitably born with the belief in one God.'[12]

To quote again from my *DNA* article:

> History offers us several confirmatory examples [of the link between monotheism, empire, imperialism and intolerance]. After the council of Nicea in 325 AD, Constantine the Great had all alternative versions of the Bible junked in order to consolidate his power. The Prophet of Islam opted for monotheism for the same reason. If people worshipped all kinds of gods, there was

> no hope in hell that they would work together. Once the rival gods were eliminated, Islam was unstoppable. Akbar, the Great, had much the same idea when he tried to create a composite religion (Din-e-elahi). He issued an 'infallibility decree' (mahzar) which said that if, in future, any questions arose relating to religious laws and their interpretation, he alone would be the final deciding authority. He got several senior ulema to sign this decree.

Hitler's Third Reich had the slogan, *Ein Volk, Ein Reich, Ein Führer* (One People, One Realm, One Leader). The only thing missing was *Ein Gott*—One God, or monotheism. Authoritarianism and intolerance need you to believe in one idea—and one idea only. And the great Abrahamic monotheisms—which believe only they have the right God and His word must rule all corners of the world—are effectively imperialisms masquerading as universalisms outside their immediate religious context.

The dilemma facing Hindus is this: to confront a universalist, imperialist and predatory idea, you cannot remain perennially divided and plural with no unity to support your independence. This means downplaying some—but not all—of the plurality, which is what gives Hinduism its uniqueness, and also the divisiveness inherent to it. Hindutva is an attempt to retain some plurality under the unifying banner of an overarching 'Hindu' identity. Beneath that identity, you can still be anything you want to be. It is a compromise between monotheism and polytheism—and an essential condition for Hindu survival.

An independent kirana shop can never win against a Walmart or an Amazon. It can choose to join one of those business ecosystems and play second fiddle, living by their rules, and survive. On its own terms, the kirana shop will be a basic survival operation.

Hindutva is the only weapon Hindus have to defeat caste-based divisiveness and disunity. Hindutva is a refusal to privilege disunity over unity. As long as predatory and imperialist faiths continue to target Hinduism for surrender, conversion or reduction to vassal status, Hindutva is an essential part of the armoury.

7

VARNA-JATI AND THE COMPLEX SYSTEM WE INHERITED

Indians, or rather Hindus, did not invent caste. What we have had is the jati, or social groups, which are not unique to Hinduism. Of course, we also had the theory of four varnas—a supposedly hierarchical system with the priestly class (Brahmins) on top, followed by warriors (Kshatriyas), the traders (Vaishyas), and the peasants and workers (Shudras).

The hierarchical nature of the varna system is often linked to the 'Purusha Sukta' of the Rig Veda, which says in its ninetieth verse in the tenth mandala (chapter or book), which was composed towards the end of the later Vedic period.

ब्राह्मणोऽस्य मुखमासीदू बाहू राजन्यः कृतः।
ऊरू तदस्य यद् वैश्यः पद्भ्याँ् शूद्रो अजायत।।

Brāhmaṇo'sya mukhamāsīd bāhū rājanyaḥ kṛtaḥ,
ūrū tadasya yad Vaiśyaḥ padbhyāgï śūdro ajāyata.

(From His face [or the mouth] came the Brahmanas. From His two arms came the rajanya [the Kshatriyas]. From His two thighs came the Vaishyas. From His two feet came the Shudras.)

Most scholars of the Rig Veda agree that this verse is a later interpolation, but regardless of this, the fact remains that some kind of hierarchy got linked to the varna concept.

Shrikant G. Talageri, who has made deep studies of the Rig Veda, especially through an understanding of linguistics, does not agree that the Purusha Sukta is an indication of a hierarchical caste system being introduced in the later Vedic age itself.

He writes in his blog:

> The basic fact is that the names for the four varṇas (social divisions of society) in the Rigveda appear only at the chronological end of the text, *and three of the words only in one single hymn*, X.90, the Puruṣha Sukta. The varṇa system is clearly a concept that arose at the fag end of the composition period of the text, at some time (between 2000 BCE and 1500 BCE) when the major part of the text had already been completed and only some latecomer compositions were being incorporated into Book 10 along with some final touches to some earlier hymns, and it is clearly an idea that was still only in the conception stage.
>
> The word varṇa itself is found twenty-three times in the Rigveda (including nine times in the Old [parts of the] Rigveda, of which two references are in a hymn in one of the three oldest books, but it is not found in *this* hymn (ie, Book 10, hymn 90). The word jāti (originally meaning 'individual endogamous tribe' from the root √jan, to be born, later renamed as 'caste' by the Portuguese) is not found *anywhere* in the whole of the Rig Veda. All this shows that the Puruṣha Sūkta, which contains this concept, was not in any way a pointer to any system of social divisions which existed in the society of

> the time, but an individual composer's *new and personal intellectual* conception of a four-fold division of human society—*any human society*.[1]

However, we don't need to argue about the origins of the verse to see what needs to be done today.

Contrary to present-day claims, jatis and varnas were initially fluid, and some of the groups often inter-married. An additional layer of complexity was introduced with the idea of *gotra* (descendants in a particular family lineage). Even within the same jati, same gotra couples could not get married. The rigidities came much later, and worsened after colonial interventions. A study conducted by the National Institute of Biomedical Genomics, West Bengal, analysed DNA evidence from 367 unrelated Indians belonging to 20 different population groups and concluded that inter-breeding slowed down around 1,600 years ago, which coincides with the Gupta period,[2] often considered the Golden Age of Hindu India. The restrictions on intercaste marriages probably began around this time, when some of the Dharmashastras were also written.

The dating seems plausible, especially since the Gupta period is widely seen as an era of rising prosperity and cultural renaissance. Rising prosperity is often linked to growing inequalities, and class and status consciousness among most populations. But if the caste system started becoming more rigid from the Gupta period, it lost in fluidity completely during colonial rule, where British census surveyors tried to force-fit each jati into a specific varna slot and found it an impossible task. Often, the difference between jati and tribe was impossible to spot, but the census surveyors went ahead and slotted jatis into predetermined or arbitrary varna slots based on dubious assumptions. The subjects' own keenness to rise in the social hierarchy through this enumeration process aided this confusion. In *Western Foundations of the Caste System*, authors Martin Fárek, Dunkin Jalki, Sufiya Pathan and Prakash Shah write:

> ...Jati refers to an entity that is neither discreet nor homogeneous. As a result, we are bound to fail in our attempt to use this as a unit of caste classification. Those who favour varna as the mode of classification face an even worse fate. Not only is it impossible to get any clear correlation between sets of jatis and varnas, with jatis constantly disputing which varnas they belong to, the added complication is that we currently have no idea how to deal with the textual sources which were taken to be the source of the theory of varna.[3]

Today's four-way classification of castes into forward castes, backward castes, scheduled castes (SCs) and scheduled tribes (STs) is largely the gift of British categorization and mis-categorization. Put simply, forced classification has led to rigid ossification over the last two hundred years.

If the caste system, or rather the varna-jati complexity, which is further complicated by ideas of gotra, is still alive and kicking, it is because jatis are repositories of social and cultural capital. Hinduism exists more in the jati traditions than in scriptures. The jati is a cohesive social group that supports its own members, both economically and socially, and thus plays a crucial role in binding people together.

As S.N. Balagangadhara told this writer in an interview,

> Jatis are social groups in Indian society. Social groups exist in all societies and in India these social groups are

> called '*jatis*'. Similar social groups that exist in societies are called differently in different parts of the world. It is as sensible to speak of 'the caste system' in India as it is to say that there is 'the social group system' in societies. Further, yes, '*Brahminism*' is an invention of western Indology.[4]

But jatis and the restrictions they may impose on individual choices can *also* be oppressive, and jatis are sometimes antagonistic to one another. While the varna hierarchy may play a role in stoking these antagonisms, very often it is jatis that are in the same geographical locations that tend to be rivals in the contest for resources and growth.

The problem in rolling varna and jati into one term called 'caste' is that it enables Hinduphobic intellectuals to eat their cake and have it too. On the one hand, they will add up all the castes to create one big 'majoritarian' idea called Hinduism, which accounts for just under 80 per cent of India's population, which is apparently out to oppress the 'minorities'. That some of these so-called 'minorities' may be more than 200 million in number does not seem to matter. However, when Hindus themselves seek to dilute the negative impact of caste-based identities by seeking a larger identity called 'Hindu' or 'Hindutva', the very same people will deny that there is anything called Hinduism, and what is there in India is just caste and discrimination.

This doublespeak enables the state to actively discriminate against Hindus and Hindu institutions, and this aspect is hard-coded into the Constitution. Article 25, which refers to the freedom to practise and propagate religion according to one's conscience, however adds caveats that largely impact Hinduism. It is interesting to note that Buddhist, Sikh and Jain temples are not run by the state, even though the Constitution lumps them together.

Article 25 reads thus:

> (1) Subject to public order, morality and health and to the other provisions of this Part, all persons are equally entitled to freedom of conscience and the right freely to profess, practise and propagate religion.
>
> (2) Nothing in this article shall affect the operation of any existing law or prevent the State from making any law—
>
> (a) regulating or restricting any economic, financial, political or other secular activity which may be associated with religious practice;
>
> (b) providing for social welfare and reform or the throwing open of Hindu religious institutions of a public character to all classes and sections of Hindus.
>
> *Explanation I.*—The wearing and carrying of kirpans shall be deemed to be included in the profession of the Sikh religion.
>
> *Explanation II.*—In sub-clause (b) of clause (2), the reference to Hindus shall be construed as including a reference to persons professing the Sikh, Jaina or Buddhist religion, and the reference to Hindu religious institutions shall be construed accordingly.

Clauses 2(a) and 2(b) are problematic for the simple reason that they allow the state to intervene wherever it believes a place of worship can be interfered with in regard to its 'secular' activities. And 2(b) ensures that in the name of justice to the SCs who were sometimes denied entry into temples and public spaces, the state can repeatedly intervene in Hindu religious institutions, even taking them over. In the Sabarimala judgment, for example, one judge used the argument of 'untouchability' to ensure that women of reproductive age should be allowed into the sanctum sanctorum of this unique shrine to Swami Ayyappa.

Some 100,000 temples are now under state control in five southern states,[5] and no state government is keen to let go—all in the name of preventing mismanagement and exclusion of some castes from entry. The fact that castes exist also among Muslims and Christians does not prevent them from running their mosques and churches autonomously. Only Hindu institutions (but not Sikh, Jain and Buddhist ones) are singled out for this treatment. Apparently, being a minority is a privileged position in India, since it gives them special rights denied to the 'majority'.

One way of guaranteeing equal rights to all religious communities is by treating all sampradayas, jatis and forest-dwelling communities as equivalent to minorities with similar rights. Right now, the state discriminates against those who think of themselves as Hindu on the specious plea that they constitute a majority, and thus need no additional constitutional guarantees on autonomy for their institutions.

On the other hand, minority institutions get the protection of Article 30(1), which says: 'All minorities, whether based on religion or language, shall have the right to establish and administer educational institutions of their choice.' This Article, meant to guarantee non-interference in minority institutions, has had the opposite effect of ensuring substantial interference in the so-called majority institutions.

The discriminatory nature of Article 30(1), at least in how it is implemented and adjudicated, is clear: it enables only minority institutions to take care of their flock autonomously, while Hindu institutions, despite being run by a diverse bunch of smaller caste and community groups, are excluded from the Article's protection. The same Article allows minority institutions to avoid obligations under the Right to Education Act, but not the so-called majority institutions. Hindu institutions thus try and create space for themselves by pretending to be linguistic minorities in regions outside their home states.

Put another way, linguistic groups have greater freedom to claim minority status if they set up shop outside their home states rather than in their home states. In the present constitutional framework, many institutions believe that their rights may best be protected by calling them minorities. This is why the Ramakrishna Mission tried, unsuccessfully, in the 1980s, to claim to be a non-Hindu denomination.[6] The Supreme Court said nothing doing a decade later.

However, this also implies that Hindu society as a whole can seldom unite to protect its collective interests in dharma. Given the importance of the jati to social cohesiveness at the grassroots, there are two ways of looking at ending the inequities inherent in varna: one is to seek the artificial annihilation of castes, as Ambedkar wanted to do at one point, and the other is to allow castes (or, rather, jatis) to flower and expand on their own by simply rejecting the hierarchical and endogamous nature of varna. Abolition of caste is not possible without mindless violence and attempts at making Hinduism uniform and fundamentalist.

The rejuvenation of Hinduism without taking on an Abrahamic character (like Sikhism did) is to make jatis the key torchbearers of varied Hinduisms. Thus, they can both preserve and expand their reach by active conversions to their caste rather than retaining a theoretical Hindu identity. The jati system carries with it a part of the DNA of the whole of Hinduism. Every jati is thus dharmic in a some way.

Critics say the problem with broad-based ghar wapsi (reconversion to Hinduism) and other religious reconversion programmes is a simple one: what caste does a potential convert convert to?[7] However, this is wrong, for organizations such as the Arya Samaj managed to reconvert without needing to slot any new convert into a specific jati or varna. Also, as Aravindan Neelakandan argues in a *Swarajya* article:

> There is room for avarna and athi-varna there: one who is outside varna and above the varna. Not only do both these categories have nothing to do with varna, they have nothing to do with jati either. More often than not, both these categories fluidly mix with each other. The foundations of Hinduism are often defined by those from this fluid category.[8]

On the other hand, if castes are at the forefront of conversion and reconversion strategies, there will be no issue. You convert to my caste, whatever it may be.

Castes became inward-looking because they encouraged endogamy and also did not allow fresh entries. This happened partly because castes were also guardians of specific vocations, whether it was the Brahmin priesthood or the Kshatriya warrior class or the Vaishya trading community or various artisan jatis. Castes thus became vehicles for retaining knowledge and intellectual property, ensuring jobs and skills within a community.

But today, professions do not stay within castes, and Brahmins can run public toilets just as Dalits can turn priests. And political power depends on castes growing larger than they currently are.

So, what does this mean? It means recognizing that caste is about kinship and social capital, and not only about hierarchies and oppression. The following ideas could offer a way forward on how reinventing castes may be important to Hindu rejuvenation.

First, jati groups must seek to convert more, and have clear entry-and-exit rules for their members. Entries and exits need not happen only through marriage and patriarchy, the latter of which will surely die at some point as women are empowered. Other criteria can and should apply too. Over time, this will ensure caste mobility, including the absorption of smaller castes into larger ones, thus giving the resultant caste larger political heft.

Second, we need to create caste councils both at the state and central levels (even district levels, since many Indian districts are larger than many countries). Conflicts and problems between castes can be addressed and resolved in these councils. The important thing to stress in this council is that all castes are equal. No caste is above another. They are just jatis, different forms of kinship.

Third, if each caste is considered almost like a separate faith group, it follows that all castes will be minorities—and thus entitled to equal rights to administer their institutions—in the Indian context. They can run their own temples and institutions, and generate resources for expanding their clout. (The other way is to amend Articles 25 to 30, so that Hindus get equal rights, as we shall discuss in another chapter. But both processes can run in parallel.)

We may be making a mistake in believing that castes are nothing but relics of the past and retrograde. They are not. Investing ourselves with guilt is a trap we need to avoid. Strengthening Hinduism needs a strengthening of jatis, but with new and inclusive architecture, with entry-and-exit rules. They may not deserve annihilation. The only caveat is that no caste is above any other caste. Another caveat: whenever we use the word 'caste', we are talking about jati, not varna.

Clearly, our understanding of castes must change, and castes themselves need to be less inward-looking than they are now.

8

WHY HINDUISM MUST BECOME A MISSIONARY RELIGION

If you are a Hindu looking to make a meaningful contribution to dharma, here's one way to make a start. Ditch those ideas that hold Hinduism back. Apart from doing something about varna-based discrimination, one idea we should not invest too much hope in is demanding a ban on religious conversions, expecting it to stop the Hindu demographic decline in India. It won't. If you are willing to give up this unworkable idea, you must necessarily adopt a corollary as your guiding principle: exhort non-Hindus to become Hindus. Hinduism must become a missionary religion once again to regain its vitality.

Before we come to the hows and whys of these two related propositions, let us understand the general idea underlying it all: nature abhors a steady state. The universe is always expanding or contracting somewhere. Life is about birthing more cells in the body than killing them. A business that intends to survive has to grow customers or write its own epitaph in slow motion. Political parties must either grow or fall apart; one that is complacent with the status quo will ultimately destroy its future. This was the reality that forced the Shiv Sena to break with the BJP in Maharashtra in 2019.

Ideas are the same. If they are not developed, nurtured and grown continuously, they will shrink and eventually die. Religions are essentially ideas with physical, emotional and psychic dimensions. If they do not seek to expand, they will shrivel, even if this trend is not clearly visible in one's own lifetime. But when it comes to a tipping point, religions may die all of a sudden. Consider what happened to Buddhism once the Islamic invasions came and destroyed their 'buts' (images of the Buddha). In *The Decline and Fall of Buddhism in India*, Ambedkar writes:

> There can be no doubt that the fall of Buddhism in India was due to the invasions of the Musalmans. Islam came out as the enemy of the 'But'. The word 'But' as everybody knows is an Arabic word and means an idol. Not many people however know what the derivation of the word 'But' is; 'But' is the Arabic corruption of Buddha. Thus the origin of the word indicates that in the Moslem mind idol worship had come to be identified with the Religion of the Buddha.[1]

Buddhism collapsed not only due to the destruction of 'buts' but also its inward focus. If Hinduism wants to escape this dismal fate at some future date, it has to act now to start growing.

Now, let's also understand why bans on religious conversions—as opposed to restrictions on the funding of proselytizing groups—are not the answer to Hinduism's steady demographic decline in India. There are already religious conversion bans in several states, but none of them has managed to stem the decline of people professing Hindu faiths.

China frowns on many official religions, including Christianity. But underground Christians are ballooning, and, by some estimates, China could well overtake the US as the world's largest Christian nation by 2030.[2] The US is the world's largest Christian nation currently, with around 230 million professing the faith, according to World Population Review estimates. China is number 10.[3]

Christianity is in decline in the US (not to speak of Europe), as more and more people have stopped practising it. About 30 per cent of all US adults now report that they follow no religion.[4] This decline of Christianity in the West is what is driving a huge push for conversions in blue-ocean countries like India.

It is also the reason why the Pope does not meet His Holiness the Dalai Lama, because the Vatican wants some say in how bishops are appointed in China,[5] a new growth area for the faith. Christians understand that if they do not grow their numbers, the faith will collapse into irrelevance. They are willing to deal with the devil (i.e. communist China) to grow.

Take another ban that hasn't worked: cow slaughter. Some 20 states across the country have banned cow slaughter, but cow smuggling and cow slaughter continue undeterred, often causing violence—even deaths—between cow smugglers and *gau rakshaks* (cow protectors). With a national cattle population of over 192 million, most of them female,[6] it is almost impossible to police cattle movements or prevent slaughter. The police have enough work on their hands preventing humans from taking to violence and crime to bother much about illegal cattle transportation and slaughter.

If this is the case with an animal which needs humans to move them around for slaughter, how successful can we be in monitoring religious conversions, when a person may convert without changing the name or even keep the knowledge within the confines of his or her home?

The only way to deter religious conversions is through intrusive policing, which no free society can allow. Even in a highly policed society (say, China), the state cannot stop you from quietly holding on to your beliefs. The courts, if anything, may not allow you to intrusively determine if someone has converted to Christianity, even if they put up a Cross on their door and go to church every Sunday.

In a case involving a woman born to Hindu parents who married a Christian, a Madras High Court bench decided that she cannot be denied SC status merely because she has adopted Christian symbols and attends church. The judgment, according to a *Times of India* report, noted:

> There is no suggestion in the [administration's] affidavit that she has abandoned her faith or that she has embraced Christianity. It is equally possible that she, as a part of a family, may accompany her husband and children for Sunday *matins*, but the *mere fact that a person goes to church* [emphasis added] does not mean that such person has altogether abandoned the original faith to which such person was born.[7]

So, while there may be a case for banning foreign contributions that aid religious conversions, banning conversions as such will be counterproductive for Hindus. There are easy ways to get around the ban. In any case, no one can be prevented from practising their new faith against their will. This leaves developing a missionary mindset as the best possible way to regenerate Hinduism.

Hindus who claim that Hinduism is not a converting faith

are probably wrong, for Hinduism could not have grown to dominate the whole of the Indian subcontinent without enough missionaries seeing it as a worthwhile idea, fit enough to practise, profess and propagate.

Consider Adi Shankaracharya. Pavan Varma, in his 2018 book on Adi Shankara, calls him 'Hinduism's foremost thinker',[8] but the first Shankaracharya was not just a thinker, but a doer and missionary. Why else would he go around the country to debate rival ideas and set up four *mutts* (religious institution or monastery) in his short 32-year lifetime to propagate Advaita?

If Hinduism had no missionaries, the ideas embedded in it would not have spread to Southeast Asia at all, where even a Muslim-majority country like Indonesia celebrates its version of the Ramayana and there is an island, Bali, which is largely Hindu.

However, the real reason why Hinduism must become a missionary religion again is that expansion and conversion strategies force you to think through your ideas, dogmas, institutions, resources and strategies. If Hindus do not build institutions, if they do not fund them and make their institutions larger than individuals, if they do not break down their faith into byte-sized ideas that the masses can easily consume, and if those ideas do not have an economic dimension which provides an incentive to convert, it cannot really survive except in niche areas confined to some parts of the world.

Currently, many Hindus make a virtue of laziness and foolishness by making the following statements about themselves. I have given the counterarguments and question the hollowness of these arguments.

1. We have survived the last 1,000 (or 5,000) years, so we will survive the next 1,000 too. Buddhism, too, was a major religion—if not the dominant one—in India for centuries. How did it suddenly disappear and allow Hinduism to become the dominant faith if the latter did not strengthen itself and spread its ideas again?

In the 1940s, South Korea was just 2 per cent Christian. In 2014, it was more than 30 per cent Christian—a 15-fold growth over three generations. But suddenly, Christianity's growth has peaked,[9] as the young have stopped attending church. Religions can grow or shrink all of a sudden when they meet, or stop meeting, the expectations of the people. When religions stop being 'cool', inspirational or dogmatic, they gradually fade.

Hinduism, too, could decline fast if it does not study demographic trends and fails to understand what keeps people loyal (or disloyal) to it. Christianity is growing in India because it has invested time and effort to understand what people want from faith.

If Hindus want to stop their demographic contraction, they have to study the weaknesses and strengths of Christianity and Islam, and create winning strategies by adopting new strengths and attacking their opponents' weaknesses. A commitment to conversion strategies automatically forces you to think along these lines. A ban on conversion allows you to relax and go to sleep and assume that there is no threat—thus enabling our enemies to gain as we slumber.

2. We give all people the freedom to follow their own ideas on faith, which means we are open and liberal. It is one thing to be open, another to be lazy and dismissive of the challenges facing the Hindu identity. Huge Muslim populations are growing in western Uttar Pradesh, West Bengal, Assam,

Kerala and coastal Karnataka around Mangalore. Christianity is spreading its wings all over the southern and tribal parts of India, not least the Northeast. Hinduism is already in retreat in these areas.

The only way to overcome this decline is by developing a commitment to grow through conversions. A religion that does not define what it offers to potential converts will not find new adherents. Existing ones may not leave due to inertia, but the young will flee.

Ask yourself: if anyone can claim to be a Hindu on their own terms without defining their relationship with dharma, then why bother becoming a Hindu at all?

However, there is another point to make as well. While it is good that Hinduism can be relatively free of dogma, it does not follow that you must not have your own set of fundamental values and propositions to offer. If Hinduism is about 'anything goes', there is no need for anyone to adopt it. It carries no clearly defined value proposition for anybody.

If Hinduism remains a do-it-yourself religion, even a Shashi Tharoor can suddenly write a book on *The Hindu Way* and no Hindu will be able to say 'bollocks'. He can define Hinduism in a way which can be self-defeating. It is good that Hinduism allows for a fair amount of customization of beliefs and practices, but if it does not develop a core, it will become an empty shell. It will be eviscerated from within.

3. All religions are the same, so what's the problem if a few Hindus convert to other religions? This is the kind of nonsense that we must stop peddling. All religions are *not* the same, and never will be, even if some points are common to them. If all religions are the same, why do Hindus convert to Christianity or Islam or even Buddhism? Why did Ambedkar make a huge political and social statement by converting to

Buddhism? If Hinduism cannot make itself relevant to those who want to leave it, it will disappear in due course.

India's 2021 census indicates a further decline in Hindu populations across almost the whole of India and a rise in Muslim demography.[10] Christian growth may be concealed as many do not openly declare their new faith for fear of losing job reservation benefits. The Hindu decline is happening because confused Hindus want to avoid commitment by claiming 'all religions are the same', thus providing the intellectual justification for inaction and defeat. A belief in '*Dilli door ast* (Delhi is a long way off)' is never a winning strategy.

4. Hinduism will not remain Hinduism if it becomes Hindutva. I define Hindutva as either political Hinduism, or an attempt to build a layer of unity among all Hindu sects and denominations. While it is true that any attempt to build unifying ideas into Hinduism will reduce some diversities, our real problem is not diversity but the glorification of disunity. Any religion that wants to survive has to build layers of unity where the diverse units can fight for their common interests, even while celebrating their differences.

Consider the case of Sikhism. The first nine Gurus were spreading the faith through reform and commitment. The ninth Guru, Tegh Bahadur, even offered his head for dharma, and the Mughal state happily took it. But offering one's head to one's enemies does not enable you to win the war for dharma. Guru Tegh Bahadur's sacrifice—one of the greatest ever—was clearly not enough to tackle the challenge of Islam in the northwest of India. It was the tenth Guru, Govind Singh, who gave Sikhism its final form and fundamentals—drawing from both Hinduism and Islam—from where the faith could not only withstand the onslaught of Islam but take the fight to it.

Did Sikhism change due to this? Yes. Could Sikhism have survived without this change? We can't say. But one thing is clear: if you choose to stand up and fight, you have to change. If you don't, you lose. You are then *forced to change* on terms set by the victors. What should one choose: changing ourselves to control our destinies, or be forced to change by those who could not care less about your faith or your heritage?

5. *Vasudhaiva Kutumbakam* (The world is one family). This phrase needs to be taken with loads of salt. The world has never been one family, and even a world run by only one religion will never be one family. The Kauravas and the Pandavas were essentially one family, but they went to war for their share of the patrimony. Dharma luckily won, but it would not have if Arjuna's weakness (he, too, believed in Vasudhaiva Kutumbakam) had not been overcome by Shri Krishna's advice to fight for dharma, as enunciated in the Gita.

Hinduism's rivals in India—Christianity and Islam—also believe in their own brand of Vasudhaiva Kutumbakam—the only difference being that it has to be under the banner of Jesus or Allah and his last Prophet. But neither Christianity nor Islam has ended wars between kingdoms and societies professing the same faith (consider Europe's world wars, and the Russia–Ukraine war, all between Christian nations), nor has Hinduism done so. *Vasudhaiva Kutumbakam is a slogan of goodwill, not strategy*. It is okay to practise family feelings when the person concerned behaves like family, not when he is planning to rob you and leave you by the wayside after sticking a knife into you.

The only way to make the world one family is for each unit of this family to be strong enough to deter the other, so that peace reigns among religions and peoples. When all religions realize that they cannot rule the world on their own terms, they will learn to work towards peace and Vasudhaiva Kutumbakam. The only guarantee of peace is effective deterrence.

To achieve Vasudhaiva Kutumbakan, Hinduism has to intellectually arm itself by becoming a missionary religion once again. As long as it stays disarmed by refusing to convert, the two desert cults, which became the top-two world religions by adopting conversion (Evangelism and Da'wa) as their guiding themes, will destroy it.

The challenge, though, is how to remain quintessentially Hindu and prevent a rigid approach to faith, as the Abrahamic religions do.

9

THE DEMOGRAPHIC CHALLENGE HINDUS FACE

Hindus (and Jains and Sikhs) in India face a demographic challenge resulting from fast-declining birth rates, and aggressive conversion strategies on the part of evangelical organizations and Islam. But the problem goes beyond just numbers, as the mainstream media and its intellectuals refuse to grasp the reality, preferring to see two other realities to suit their ideological biases: one is the fast decline in Muslim fertility rates and the other is the static (and misleading) share of Christians in the Indian population, as shown in the 2011 Census numbers.[1] The Christian share of India's population, according to the Census, is 2.3 per cent, but some recent investigations by Surendranath C. (explained later) show that the real numbers may be higher.[2]

The last National Family Health Survey (NFHS-5) (2019–21) showed a sharp decline in Muslim total fertility rates (TFRs) compared to other religions, giving ammunition to 'Left-liberals' to dub all Hindu fears about adverse demographic change as just 'Hindutva propaganda'.[3]

S.Y. Quraishi, a former chief election commissioner

and author of the book *The Population Myth: Islam, Family Planning and Politics in India*, wrote in *The Times of India*, that Muslims are not averse to family planning.[4] The idea that the Muslim population will overtake that of Hindus is plain wrong, he claims. Using mathematical models, he says the Muslim population can never overtake that of Hindus in India.

Swaminathan, Anklesaria Aiyar has much the same thing to say. In an article written in *The Times of India*, he makes three arguments to pooh-pooh Hindu concerns over adverse demographic changes. First, even assuming the Muslim proportion rises at the same rate that it has since 1951 (a 4.4 per cent rise over six decades), it won't be more than 20 per cent by 2100 CE. Two, the Hindu–Muslim birth rate differential is falling, with fertility rate gaps falling from 1.1 (additional child) per woman to 0.5 between 1992 and 2015. This means that the total fertility rate differential will become zero in two decades. And, three, the difference in levels of poverty (higher among Muslims) explains the current hiatus between Muslim and Hindu fertility rates.[5]

With regard to Christians, Aiyar makes the claim that their population share in India has stayed at 2.3 per cent between 1951 and 2015, and hence poses no demographic threat.

However, this is unlikely to be true, and the Census figures may not capture ground realities where conversions to Christianity are significant in many states. One can see this in the aggressive church-building activities in southern India, especially in Tamil Nadu and Andhra Pradesh, where their actual numbers are probably being under-reported.

We shall later debunk the arguments that Hindus are exaggerating the demographic challenge, but for now, let us focus on what Hindus are doing wrong: they are simply unable to articulate what the real demographic concerns are, and making things worse by calling on Hindu women to produce more children. Mindless rants from sants at some Dharam Sansad or the other, calling on Hindu women to produce four to five children each to make up for lower birth rates, has only helped Hinduphobes erect strawman arguments against Hindutva and demolish them convincingly. Not only are such calls misogynistic, for every woman has a right to decide along with her spouse how many children she wants to have, but what matters is not just the raw numbers but the quality of those numbers. Producing more kids and then allowing them to suffer poverty and deprivation is hardly the best way to arrest adverse demographic trends.

The real problem is not Hindutva propaganda, as secular critics are claiming, but very poor articulation of their demographic concerns by them and a data-illiterate media.

The latest NFHS-5 (2019–21) shows that Muslim TFRs have fallen by 46.5 per cent since NFHS-1 (1992–93) compared to 41.2 per cent for Hindus.[6] Most newspapers highlighted this aspect to tell us that Muslim birth rates are falling faster than that of Hindus. What they miss out is a simple statistical fact: when the base is high, percentage changes tend to get exaggerated. Muslim TFRs were super high at 4.41 in NFHS-1, while the Hindu TFR was 3.3. What they also miss out is the reality that even after the sharp fall, Muslims are the *only* community still above-replacement levels of TFR (2.36 versus Hindu levels of 1.94, against replacement levels of 2.1 live births per woman). In comparative terms, Muslims will keep raising their share of population for at least one or two decades. Hindu growth rates will shrink, while Muslim ones will expand in the foreseeable future.

Let us further examine what 'liberals' have been saying to deny any basis for Hindu concerns. Apart from the three arguments mentioned earlier, Aiyar also throws in claims that immigration from Pakistan and Bangladesh cannot be causing a demographic surge among Muslims. Then, he tosses in a red herring to put Hindus on the defensive. He says that taboos on widow remarriage among Hindus may have restrained Hindu birth rates. But this is unlikely to be substantially true, for if the critical reason for a falling birth rate is the non-availability of unmarried (or widowed) women to produce more children, one can say the same about polygamy. If some men are entitled to four wives, this should reduce the availability of women to the rest of the population, and hence curtail birth rates. Unless the argument is that polygamous males will make up for the deficit. But wasn't this the exact argument that was debunked by the same 'liberals' to claim that polygamy is not responsible for high birth rates among the Muslim population in India?

In fact, data about gender ratios at birth show that till the late 1960s, India produced 1.05 boys per girl child, which is close to the global average. It is only after our leaders started fretting about population control (*'Hum do, hamare do* [Two of us, two of ours]') and technology made prenatal sex determination tests widely available that the gender ratios started skewing in favour of boys. So, taboos around widow remarriage, which were stronger in the 1950s and 1960s than they are now, can hardly be blamed for this differential fertility rate today.

This brings us to the larger issue of loss of Hindu demography. But our faux liberals need to be educated on some basics first.

In principle, it is wrong to lump all of India in one bucket to say Hindus have no reason for concern. The partition of India on religious lines is proof that whenever Hindu demography deteriorates in any region, it impacts Hindu rights and prompts Hindu migration away from that region. We have seen this happening not only in Pakistan and Bangladesh but also inside India itself, in Kashmir; and this may be quietly happening in other districts which have seen increases in Muslim populations. These include districts in north Kerala, Assam, West Bengal and parts of Bihar and Uttar Pradesh, among others. Hindu concerns are valid if demography is adversely affected in any state or district of India. One cannot use data for the whole of India to invalidate Hindu concerns.

Secondly, demography is impacted not only by differential fertility rates but immigration, too. Aiyar makes the point that out-migration is higher among Muslims than Hindus, with 27 per cent of total out-migration (compared to the population share of 14.2 per cent) compared to 45 per cent for Hindus (who form 79.8 per cent of the population). On the other hand, he estimates that inflows from Bangladesh are barely 3.2 million so far, against 1.1 million from Pakistan.[7] So, net-net, Muslims are migrating out more than in.

This is a dubious claim and goes against the available evidence. Out-migration can be of two types: those who leave India for good and those who leave India for short-term jobs. Most of the Muslim out-migrants are likely to be those who found lucrative jobs in the Muslim parts of the Gulf, who don't easily give Indians citizenship and hence they may not be permanent emigres. In the wake of the Covid-19 economic collapse, many Indians working in the Gulf lost their jobs and were seeking new options back home.[8]

As for the claim that only 3.2 million came to India from Bangladesh,[9] the demographic evidence is to the contrary. If only 3.2 million came from Bangladesh, and even assuming most of them were Hindus fleeing an Islamized society, how does this explain the drastic fall of Hindu numbers from 22.03 per cent of the population in 1951 (the first Census of East Pakistan) to just 8.54 per cent now? Equally, if more Hindus than Muslims migrated out of Bangladesh, there should be a corresponding increase in Hindu proportions in West Bengal and Assam, but nothing of that kind happened. What really may have happened is, apart from fertility differentials, the proportion of Muslims migrating out of Bangladesh was almost as high as Hindus fleeing persecution. In Assam, the share of the Hindu population has fallen from 73.32 per cent in 1951 to 62.04 per cent in 2011, while that of Muslims went up from 24.8 per cent to 34.22 per cent during the same period.[10]

In West Bengal, the share of Hindus fell from nearly 80 per cent in 1991 to just over 72 per cent in 2011, with the Muslims making solid gains. Their share rose from 19.5 per cent to 27 per cent, and current estimates are that the real numbers could be closer to 30 per cent.[11]

If this is not significant demographic change in just over three decades, what is?

Third, the argument that poverty explains most of the difference in religious fertility rates cannot be true everywhere. In Kerala, where Muslims form 26.56 per cent of the population and are not educationally or economically backward compared to Hindus, it was discovered that 41.45 per cent of live births in 2015 were children born to Muslims. The Hindu birth rate was down to 42 per cent, far lower than their share of Kerala's population.

Says a *Business Standard* report from September 2017:

> [The] share of Muslims in the child (0-6yr) population of Kerala and [...] in live births in the state are much higher than their share in the population and have been

> rising rapidly. Muslims have a share of 41.45 percent in the live births in 2015 compared to 36.32 percent in 2008. And they have a share of 36.74 percent in the 0-6 population of the state in 2011 compared to 31.08 percent in 2001. Their share in the total population, as counted in Census 2011, is only 26.56 percent.[12]

This has led some people to surmise that Hindus could fall below 50 per cent over the next one or two censuses in Kerala, since Christians form another 19 per cent of the population. And is this not a major demographic change, where a majority becomes a minority within living memory?

Fourth, demography changes not only due to fertility differences and immigration but also aggressive conversion activities by Muslims and Christians. Aiyar's claim that the Christian population of India has stayed at 2.3 per cent between 1951 and 2015 is questionable, and the Census figures may not fully capture ground realities on recent conversions to Christianity in several states. One can see this in the aggressive church-building activities in southern India, especially in Tamil Nadu and Andhra Pradesh, where their actual numbers may be under-reported, as mentioned earlier.

An analysis by Surendranath C. for *Swarajya* shows that in post-bifurcation Andhra Pradesh, the number of Christians (according to the 2011 Census) is just around 6.8 lakh.[13] But memberships claimed by organized churches in the state reveal a Christian population of at least 50–60 lakh, which will be around 12 per cent of the state's population. If the estimate has erred by a factor of two, the proportions would be 25 per cent, which was the percentage claimed by a YSR Congress MP, Raghu Ramakrishna Raju, in an interview around mid-2020.[14]

What explains this divergence between official census figures and the real figures after accounting for conversions? The assumption is that many Christians declare themselves as Hindus to benefit from reservations for the SC/ST.

Surendranath, in his article for *Swarajya*, makes this point through the example of Guntur district in Andhra Pradesh. He writes:

> The trends in the report [by the Centre for Policy Studies]...shows some very curious trends. The Christian population in Guntur district alone was 14.2 percent in 1971 but has declined to less than 1 percent in 2011, or from 4.2 lakh to just 90,000 in absolute numbers. On the other hand, the share of Scheduled Castes (SCs) in the population of Guntur district rose from 4.8 percent in 1971 to 19.59 percent in 2011.[15]

India's faux liberals need to open their eyes to reality and engage with real Hindu concerns over demographic change instead of building strawman arguments and denying the reality.

However, one good that has come out of all these arguments is this: there is now an indirect admission that demographic change on some scale is unwelcome. Otherwise, why would they resort to bogus arguments to deny this is happening? Truth dawns on liberals a bit too slowly for our comfort, but truth has an uncomfortable way of bobbing up in front of even those who are unwilling to see it.

But Hindus also need to articulate their concerns better without hyperbole. Here are the real arguments they should use:

1. Demography is impacted not just by TFR but also by two other factors: conversion and immigration. Till recently,

Hindus did not bother to create an ecosystem for conversions, while Islam and Christianity have always had them. Even after ghar wapsi programmes, the Hindu conversion machinery is simply unequal to the task of meeting the challenges posed by churches and mosques.

India also has porous borders on the east. The possibility of climate change impacting Bangladesh more than India, and aggressive actions against Muslim minorities in Myanmar, could conceivably bring in more Muslim immigrants to India. Assam did not move from a Muslim population of 30.9 per cent to 34.2 per cent between 2001 and 2011 just because of higher TFRs among Muslims in the state.

Net result: demography will change adversely for Hindus in the Northeast and some other parts of India. So, while talking demographic shifts, don't ignore the issues of aggressive conversion activities and illegal immigration.

2. The demographic threat relates not only to Muslims but also Christians. Hindus tend to talk more about the Muslim threat because of their historical experiences with bigoted Muslim rulers, who demolished temples and organized forced conversions. Their thinking has also been impacted by the pre-Independence Congress party's total inability to get a buy-in from Muslims on secularism, resulting in Partition. The Khilafat movement, the atrocities of the Moplahs against Hindus in the Malabar, Jinnah's Direct Action Day, the murder of Arya Samaj leader Swami Shraddhanand by a Muslim fanatic, and the ethnic cleansing of Hindus from Pakistan, Bangladesh and our own Kashmir have made Hindus more fearful of Muslim intentions than Christians, whereas demographically both threaten Hindu numbers.

3. Demography can be impacted by structural flaws in how data is collected and/or confirmed, which may result

in serious undercounting of some minority religious groups and overcounting of Hindus. Very often, Hindus are defined not by which religion they actually follow but who they are not: if you are not Muslim, Christian, Buddhist, Jain or Sikh, you are assumed to be Hindu. In short, Hindus are often 'none-of-the-above' people. One wonders whether atheists like communists, and anti-Hindu groups like Dravidian racists can be counted as Hindu when they are manifestly not Hindu by faith, and often make Hinduphobic political statements in the name of opposing casteism or Brahminism.

Christians may also be seriously undercounted, for their population share has remained almost static at 2.3 per cent since Independence. This contrasts sharply with the aggressive funding for conversion activities, including frenetic church-building in the South, over the last decade or so, as the investigation by Surendranath C. for *Swarajya* shows.

Christians may be undercounted because they have an incentive to do so: if they declare themselves Hindu, they get all the benefits of affirmative action, including reserved seats in educational institutions and jobs in government services. So, why declare yourself a Christian and lose these benefits?

4. It is a mistake to take Muslim and Christian numbers on an all-India basis, when the real demographic threat is at the level of some states and regions within states. The Muslim or Christian demographic threat is real in Assam, Kerala, Tamil Nadu, Andhra Pradesh, West Bengal, parts of eastern Bihar that are near the Bangladesh border and western Uttar Pradesh. If we take district-wise religious population shares, the picture will be bear out many Hindu concerns in contrast to when we take India as a whole.

5. Given the porosity of borders, the demographic threat in the Indian subcontinent (i.e. taking India, Pakistan and

Bangladesh together) is much greater than when we take India alone. In 1941, before Partition, India's Muslim population was around 27 per cent and Hindus around 65 per cent. But 27 per cent could force a Partition. Today, the Muslim share is closer to 32 per cent in the subcontinent. In Assam, West Bengal, Kerala and western Uttar Pradesh, the Muslim population share is at or above Muslim shares in pre-Partition India. This percentage reinforces Hindu fears that Muslim numbers are reaching levels where unreasonable demands could be made in the name of secularism or minority rights that will impact national cohesion or unity. Terrorism from Pakistan has not helped matters.

6. Global majorities matter more than just a local majority. Christianity and Islam constitute global majorities, with over 100 and 50 countries being Christian- and Muslim-majority countries, respectively. Thus, the share of global voice of these two Abrahamic religions is enormous, while Hindus, who constitute the third-largest religious group globally but are largely confined to India, have only one country to speak for them. And even here, speaking for Hindu rights is silenced in the name of secularism. If Hindus cannot maintain an effective share of dominance in India, the long-term consequences for a religion that does not proselytize or have an imperial vision will always be negative.

Hindu demographic fears are not just about numbers. They emanate from the nature of the challenges posed by two expansionist, predatory and imperialistic visions of faith that Islam and Christianity represent. The resources that these two faiths can pour into India simply dwarf what Hindus are capable of, especially when the sources of religious wealth (i.e. temples) are often in state hands. The dice are loaded against Hindus.

10

LOVE JIHAD AND OTHER ISSUES

One Hindu fear which is partly imaginary and partly real relates to what is pejoratively called Love Jihad, which loosely means Muslim men targeting Hindu women for marriage and conversion to Islam. For 'liberals', there is no such thing as Love Jihad, and that it is merely love driving interfaith marriages.

Without actual data on whether these are fringe phenomenon or something more significant, we cannot comment on how serious this form of demographic threat is. However, it is fair to say that five asymmetries load the dice against any two-way trends where the numbers converting to Islam are matched by those converting to Hinduism through the institution of marriage, as I wrote in *Swarajya* in November 2020.[1]

Faced with news reports about Muslims misrepresenting themselves as Hindus to woo Hindu girls for marriage and conversions, states like Uttar Pradesh have enacted laws to prevent Love Jihad. But, so far, courts have not intervened to stop this misrepresentation, and the laws intended to curb this practice may also face rejections or modifications by courts, many of whom have refused to intervene, claiming that they cannot prevent women from making their own choices. The fact is, no law can prevent conversions during marriage unless society vaccinates itself against this outcome, just as anti-conversion laws cannot work unless society arms itself to both defend its numbers and gain converts from rival religions. Hindus have done neither.

Hindus face five asymmetries of power when it comes to Christianity and Islam, and if they do not adopt countermeasures, these asymmetries will ultimately affect them demographically in India—the only major country where Hindus are in majority.

The first asymmetry to address is the attitude to conversion and weak institutional mechanisms in Hinduism to remedy this. You cannot expect to stem the outflow of Hindus to other religions if you do not have a conversion or reconversion strategy that can be scaled up to meet the challenges posed by two expansionist religions.

In the battle for numbers, the two Abrahamic religions come with money, resources and institutional strengths to advance their causes, while Hindus are left to defend themselves unarmed. This is a losing strategy. You cannot fight guns with bare hands, or with a law that merely outlaws guns but cannot be enforced. But this is essentially what Hindus are trying to do.

If two religions are primed to seek converts, and the target religion is not equipped even to defend itself, what other outcome can there be but defeat?

The second asymmetry to address is patriarchy. All religions are patriarchal, and Islam is (arguably) more so than any other. But Hinduism alone is driven by sheer naivete, where we are increasingly wise enough to educate our girls to get jobs but not hard-headed enough to educate them about their rights if they enter into interfaith marriages. Worse, if a Hindu woman fights for her religious identity or gender rights in such a marriage, Hindu society will not even rush to help them, and our politicians and courts will steer clear of 'communalism'.

The courts are equally naive in this matter. In one Allahabad High Court case, the bench made the following motherhood statement:

> We do not see Priyanka Kharwar and Salamat as Hindu and Muslim, rather as two grown-up individuals who, out of their own free will and choice, are living together peacefully and happily (for) over a year...The courts and the Constitutional courts in particular are enjoined to uphold the life and liberty of an individual guaranteed under Article 21 of the Constitution of India. Right to live with a person of his/her choice irrespective of [the] religion professed by them is intrinsic to right to life and personal liberty. Interference in a personal relationship would constitute a serious encroachment into the right to freedom of choice of the two individuals.[2]

The problem with this statement is not its constitutional intent, but what it ignores in terms of the underlying social reality. A woman who defies her family to marry outside her caste or religion effectively has to make peace with her husband's family, failing which she will be left neither here nor there. If she asserts her religious identity in an interfaith marriage, she may face covert or overt pressures to abandon them, and her children may also face discrimination.

In a patriarchal society, women in general are forced to adjust to their spouses' culture and practices; what is the probability that Priyanka will be able to retain her Hindu identity and individualism even if she wanted to?

Even in cases where, say, a Muslim boy falsely represents himself as Hindu and then, after cohabitation, decides to reveal that he is not Anand but Ahmed, which woman will have the courage to turn away and fight for her rights against the cheat, given the amount of emotional investment she has in the relationship?

Even rape victims sometimes agree to marry their tormentors in order to salvage something of their lives, so it is highly unlikely that a Priyanka will have the courage to hold on to her identity—conversion or no conversion. In Indian society, it is easier for a man to hold on to his identity in an interfaith marriage than a woman. Patriarchy ensures that interfaith marriages are loaded against the woman more than the man.

The third asymmetry relates to personal laws and social customs. For Hindus, marriage ceremonies are about the traditions and rituals to be followed; they do not imply any conversion. In a *niqah* or a church wedding officiated by a Christian priest, conversion is mandatory before such weddings take place.

The only way the law can help is if personal laws are reduced to mere social constructs with no legal sanctity; bigamy also needs to be outlawed—personal law or no personal law. This will protect both Muslim and Hindu women on their marital rights, whether the marriage is within the same faith or interfaith. But, clearly, women, especially Hindu women, need to be educated on what they lose by agreeing to a niqah or a church wedding. Hindu society has to empower them to make the right choices with open eyes, and not make them fall into a trap they did not see when they married someone from another religion who they liked.

The fourth asymmetry relates to Muslim women and the community male's attitudes to them. Many wear full-face burkhas and others cover their heads with a hijab. Both types of women are also culturally warned to stay away from men, especially the ones outside their faith. Thus, while Muslim men can meet up with Hindu women and date them fairly easily, a burkha-clad Muslim woman or girl is—by definition—declaring herself to be out of bounds for men and boys from another community. Very few non-Muslims will feel emboldened enough to approach Muslim girls and young women for even a casual meeting, leave alone a date.

This asymmetry can be addressed only if Muslim society modernizes and changes its own patriarchal attitudes towards women, but that is a far cry right now. In the foreseeable future, this asymmetry will remain.

Ambedkar had strong words to describe the purdah system as a huge social evil in his tract on Pakistan. He wrote:

> As a consequence of the *purdah* system, a segregation of the Muslim women is brought about. The ladies are not expected to visit the outer rooms, verandahs, or gardens; their quarters are in the back-yard. All of them, young and old, are confined in the same room. No male servant can work in their presence. A woman is allowed to see only her sons, brothers, father, uncles, and husband, or any other near relation who may be admitted to a position of trust. She cannot go even to the mosque to pray, and must wear *burka* (veil) whenever she has to go out. These *burka* women walking in the streets is one of the most hideous sights one can witness in India. Such seclusion cannot but have its deteriorating effects

> upon the physical constitution of Muslim women [...] *Purdah* deprives Muslim women of mental and moral nourishment [...]
>
> They lag behind their sisters from other communities, cannot take part in any outdoor activity and are weighed down by a slavish mentality and an inferiority complex [...]
>
> The evil consequences of *purdah* are not confined to the Muslim community only. It is responsible for the social segregation of Hindus from Muslims which is the bane of public life in India. This argument may appear far-fetched, and one is inclined to attribute this segregation to the unsociability of the Hindus rather than to *purdah* among the Muslims. *But the Hindus are right when they say that it is not possible to establish social contact between Hindus and Muslims, because such contact can only mean contact between women from one side and men from the other* [last emphasis added].[3]

The fifth asymmetry relates to who Muslim society considers a Muslim and its harsh rules on apostasy. As Nassim Nicholas Taleb writes in his book, *Skin in the Game*, Muslim demographic growth is aided by the following two asymmetric rules. First, under Islamic law, if a non-Muslim marries a Muslim woman, he needs to convert to Islam—and if either parent of the child happens to be Muslim, the child will be Muslim. Second, becoming Muslim is irreversible, as apostasy is the heaviest crime in the religion, sanctioned by the death penalty.[4]

If Hindus are to hold their own, leave alone win, in the battle of demography, they have to understand these asymmetries and find answers to them. Islam and Christianity are like 'Hotel California': anyone can enter, but none (or few) can leave (easily). Hinduism is the exact opposite: anyone can leave, but few can enter easily.

Laws cannot rectify this asymmetry beyond a point. It is for society to recognize the problem and deal with it.

11

CREATING A HINDU ECOSYSTEM FOR CONVERSION

Two high-profile conversions to Hinduism in 2021, one in India and the other in Indonesia, have been welcomed by many Hindus with relief, for it signals a small reversal of the trend of Hindus moving away to Abrahamic faiths. However, these cases should prompt Hindus and Hindu organizations to ask themselves a fundamental question: do they have the necessary ecosystem to support ghar wapsi and formal conversions of people who were never Hindu on a wider scale than now?

In Indonesia, former President Sukarno's daughter, Sukmawati Sukarnoputri, left Islam to become Hindu in October 2021.[1] Later that year, a former chairman of the Uttar Pradesh Shia Wakf Board, Waseem Rizvi, was converted to Hinduism by Swami Yati Narsinghanand, head priest of the Dasna Devi temple in Ghaziabad, and renamed Jitendra Narayan Singh Tyagi.[2] Bounties were offered for Rizvi's head soon after.[3]

In March 2021, Rizvi received a huge backlash from Muslim organizations when he moved a public interest litigation in the Supreme Court seeking the deletion of 26 verses from the Koran which were anti-kafir. The petition was dismissed by a bench headed by Justice Rohinton Nariman, who claimed it was frivolous and imposed costs on Rizvi.[4] The court declined to act on a petition that sought exclusion of some of the Muslim holy book's illiberal verses.

Not that any judiciary can edit a holy book, but the least the Supreme Court could have done was make positive comments on the need to review those verses by Muslims themselves. But that's another story.

What is material here is the fact that Hindu society does not have the ability to protect the new convert, and demanding state protection from Islamic fanatics who are willing to die in their cause is not feasible on a large scale if ghar wapsi is to be pursued beyond one or two high-profile cases. The state could not protect Kamlesh Tiwari in 2019, who allegedly blasphemed against the Prophet, from his alleged Muslim assassins.[5] Death threats against a former BJP spokesperson, Nupur Sharma, who also allegedly blasphemed against the Prophet during a TV show in June 2022, continue, with Muslim groups taking to the streets shouting '*sar tan se juda* (a call to sever the head from the body, i.e. a beheading)'. The Supreme Court was forced to offer some legal relief in the face of these unceasing death threats.[6]

Worse, Hindu society at large does not even know how to help new converts adjust to Hinduism—though the Vishwa Hindu Parishad and some of the Sangh's front organizations do report some success in this regard.

An ecosystem for encouraging ghar wapsi and conversions of members belonging to non-Hindu societies (say, in America, Europe or Latin America) needs a solid support structure.

One, there needs to be a formal system of training priests

and *pracharak*s who are aware of the basics of Hinduism and know how to approach potential crossover members from another community.

Two, the wider society at large should be educated on how the new converts need to be treated and helped to adjust to their new religion, rituals and practices. On the contrary, many Hindus probably have a suspicious attitude to new converts, and even quickly write off people who convert away from Hinduism. If this was not the case, one wonders what stopped Hindus who were forcibly converted by Tipu Sultan, or by the Moplahs in 1921, from reconverting them once the scourges were dealt with by the British and other law enforcers.

Forced conversions are usually reversible in the first generation as the converts would normally be unhappy over the use of force to obtain their loyalties for a new faith. But this return can happen only if their old faiths are willing to accept them back, but Hindus have often raised taboos about those returning to the fold, especially if they have been forced to consume beef or are circumcised. In the case of evangelical Christianity or Islam, ordinary members of the communities go all out to support new converts. There are also penalties and incentives in place to prevent new converts from slipping back into their old religions.

Three, a proper ecosystem should include plans to retain the members beyond one or two generations. Many churches, for example, allow first-generation interfaith marriages to continue without conversion (i.e. if the non-Christian partner insists on it), but they do ask the family to ensure that any children born in this marriage must be raised as Christians. In Islam, there is no such thing as an interfaith marriage; if you accept a nikah ceremony, you are deemed to be a

Muslim, and your children will be raised in that faith. This happens because both Christianity and Islam know that till a conversion is confirmed in the succeeding generations, it remains tentative.

Fourth, we cannot wish away the reality that converts may be seeking more than just spiritual and dogmatic guidance. Easier admissions to schools run by the new faith, or support to find employment are equally important drivers of conversions (or retentions within a faith). One can deride them as 'rice-bag' converts, but we cannot deny that material benefits are important incentives for conversion in the first generation. Once the second and third generations remain in the faith, the investment in new converts becomes self-supporting, for these generations start contributing to churches and religious causes.

This fact alone tells us how important it is to wrest back control of temples from the state, and insist on autonomy for Hindu-run institutions.

The only way Hindu demography can be maintained or expanded in India is by making Hinduism a missionary faith, but this means creating an ecosystem to support such missionary activities. Islam and Christianity are leagues ahead of Hindus in this race. If we don't start building this ecosystem now, the two Abrahamic faiths will gain at our cost. Hinduism will shrivel and wither in the land of its birth.

12

THE CASE FOR HINDUISM LITE

A key strength, and critical weakness, of Hinduism is that it is too much of a do-it-yourself religion, one where individuals can decide who they want to worship, which rituals they want to follow and how high (or low) to aim for when it comes to matters spiritual. They have not stopped to ask themselves why some Hindus find a crossover to the Abrahamic religions worth their while, despite the richness of their own Hindu and dharmic heritage.

It is best to understand the overall religious conversion scenario as a marketplace—a marketplace for religious products and consumers. In this market, Christianity is the leader, Islam the challenger brand (a Pepsi fighting Coca-Cola for leadership), and Hinduism and other religions the niche players, even though Hindu numbers are the third largest in the world. In Hinduism, it's not the overall numbers that matter. Each sampradaya behaves like a separate niche product.

When Coca-Cola and Pepsi battle it out, it is the smaller players that are squeezed out since market share for the big two can be grown only by focussing on winning converts from the smaller players.

India and China are the biggest markets for growth of Product Bible and Product Koran. China is a closed market, and growth can happen only surreptitiously, and that leaves only India as the biggest market worth exploiting.

The other reality of the marketplace is segmentation. Religious products have to appeal to different segments of the market—the high end, the middle end and the low end—to break it up into simple chunks.

Christianity and Islam, with their emphasis on the less fortunate and justice, appeal to the lowest end of the mass market, while Indic religions, by their high metaphysical content, tend to appeal to the upper and middle segments. The bottom end has sometimes been addressed, as in the case of the Bhakti movements that started in the mediaeval period, but this hasn't been consistent.

In the 1980s, Hindustan Unilever's Surf was the detergent market leader, but it was too expensive for the masses. Karsanbhai Patel saw an opportunity for Nirma and took away large market shares from Surf. To retain share, Hindustan Unilever had to launch a mass-market brand called Wheel, and has not looked back since.

On the other hand, the upper-end market is also expanding, which explains the Ariels and Henkos jostling for space. In the sphere of spirituality, there is also a growing market for upper-end metaphysics. The rich West is actually the best market for growing Brand Hinduism or Brand Buddha. Reason: it has less of poverty, and once humans are relieved of basic insecurities involving survival and safety, they have a greater need for intellectual stimulation that takes you beyond narrow religious dogma—which was what helped the Abrahamic faiths to spread fast among the masses. The West may be seeking an upgrade, and this is the market Hindu seers need to address.

It is not that Christian theologists are not aware of this. This is why they are trying to 'digest' Hindu-Buddhist-dharmic ideas and still call it Christianity. Hence, you have 'Christian yoga'[1], and a whole raft of Christian evangelists, theologists and ministers hawking new, improved versions of Christianity, which involve less dogmatic interpretations of the Bible. They draw a lot from dharmic metaphysics. For example, Neale Donald Walsch's various books on 'Conversations with God' have little of the core Christian dogmas of virgin birth or the rubbishing of other spiritual traditions. Indians buy his books as though they are new revelations, when it is their own spiritual traditions they have lost touch with.

In order to tackle the 'Surf' end of the religion market, new Christian evangelists (or even those like Walsch, who are not stuck on Christianity as the only way) use the West's latest knowledge in marketing, human psychology, sociology and competitor products to reposition their faith and target all ends of the market—from the top end to the bottom. For its home market, which has evolved beyond dogma, Christianity uses Indic and other ideas to develop products. For mass markets like India, where social tension and poverty are ever-present realities, the evangelists and even Islamic ulema can use their old marketing strategies that are aggressive and sometimes more socially relevant. In simple terms, as things stand, the Indic spiritual or religious products are ideal for developed western markets and the Christian or Islamic products are easier to peddle in the Indian market.

If Hinduism has to hold its own in the home market

and also explore new markets, it has to have at least two products: a sophisticated version for the western markets, which modern-day gurus like Sri Sri Ravi Shankar and Sadhguru Jaggi Vasudev are clearly delivering, and a Hinduism Lite (or a new form of Hinduism for the masses, possibly created under the banner of Hindutva) for India, where the social content (strong anti-caste stand, social welfare, women's emancipation, etc.) is emphasized more than high metaphysics.

In a sense, Hindutva is a move in this direction, and has even succeeded to some extent, given that it is now dominated by other backward classes (OBCs) and not the upper castes, but it is simply not focussed enough to deliver a big-ticket mass market product. While the building of a Ram temple in Ayodhya is targeting all segments, as is the focus on reclaiming the Kashi and Mathura holy sites, the focus on banning cow slaughter and forcing people not to eat beef cannot help. These are not always the primary concerns of the mass market for Hinduism in India. And hence, Hindutva in its current form is bound to face challenges to growth. Vegetarianism and veganism are upper-end concerns.

If Hinduism Lite is to succeed, it needs to be more radical on social messaging and become simpler in terms of the expected spirituality of its target audience, which is just past the survival or basic needs stage. It is about having clarity on core ideas (even dogmas). In some ways, the International Society for Krishna Consciousness (ISKCON) is structured a bit like Hinduism Lite, where it uses Abrahamic ideas of one true god (Shri Krishna, around whom all other Hindu avatars are linked). A.C. Bhaktivedanta Swami Prabhupada, the founder of ISKCON, is its prophetic Guru, and the Bhagavad Gita is their central religious text. It helps that in the

Gita, Shri Krishna reveals himself as the creator of everything and the only one who can dissolve sins and offer moksha.

Chapter 18, Verse 66 of the Gita reads:

> सर्वधर्मान्परित्यज्य मामेकं शरणं व्रज ।
> अहं त्वां सर्वपापेभ्यो मोक्षयिष्यामि मा शुचः ।।66।।
>
> *Sarva-dharmān parityajya mām ekaṁ śharaṇaṁ vraja*
> *ahaṁ tvāṁ sarva-pāpebhyo mokṣhayiṣhyāmi mā śhuchaḥ*
>
> (Abandon all dharmas and seek refuge in me
> I will liberate you from all sin and give you moksha.)

But ISKCON is not the only workable idea of Hinduism Lite, though it is missionary in its objective, including the objective of conversion from other faiths (a vital property of Hinduism Lite). Many more are needed. But, most important, Hinduism Lite has to develop a sophisticated way of dealing with rivals, and not the attitude of a fearful lynch mob.

Consider how the sophisticated anti-Hindu lobby is dealing with the rise of Sri Sri Ravi Shankar. Some years ago, they attacked his World Culture Festival on the banks of the Yamuna by talking about environmental damage,[2] and not in the usual way the Hindutva crowd attacks rivals, with unparliamentary words and angry thoughts.

Sadhguru Jaggi Vasudev is constantly targeted about his land acquisition around Coimbatore by liberals and evangelical groups.[3] This is partly because Tamil Nadu is home to Dravidianism and anti-Brahminism, which is often Hinduphobic. Though Sadhguru claims to be self-taught on his spiritual philosophy, it is rooted in dharmic ideas. That's one red rag to the secular crowd. The opposition to him is not directly about his ideas, but through indirect means.

Hinduphobes, calling themselves 'liberals', target Diwali, Jallikattu (a sport involving taming a bull), Kambala (an annual buffalo race held in coastal Karnataka) and even Dahi Handi (the making of human pyramids to crack the pot of curd during Shri Krishna Jayanti) using social justice concepts such as child and animal rights, not to speak of pollution.

Some Muslims have opposed the Amarnath Yatra by saying that too many people visiting that shrine will damage the environment.[4] They would never say this about the millions of Muslims doing the haj, which causes more environmental damage than almost any Hindu pilgrimage.[5] So, the next attack by Hinduphobes can easily be expected—the Kumbh Mela will be shown as anti-environment, as Rajiv Malhotra has documented in a tract.[6]

The Christian West masks its subtle Hinduphobia by generating and spreading horror stories about rapes, caste violence and other kinds of 'atrocity' literature.[7] They are as racist and judgmental as they have always been, but they use new terms to achieve their old objective of dominance—by taking up issues related to the environment, women's empowerment, freedom of religion, free speech and 'liberal' values. Racism and colonialism are surfacing in a new garb, speaking a new modern language that is difficult to refute directly.

Meanwhile, the India-based Hinduphobic elite uses colonial era divide-and-rule tactics to achieve the same end. When Hinduphobes seek to demonize those who try to organize Hindus, they will talk about the ancient Hindu attitude of tolerance to show that real Hinduism is different from Hindutva. This Hinduphobic elite became self-loathing for the same reason some others became part of the violent

Hindu fringe—by internalizing colonial era anti-Hindu critiques and developing a sense of inferiority. Those who internalized this negativity about Hinduism became either Hinduphobic or violent Hindu fringe elements.

Consider also the sophisticated way in which Left and secular historians end up saying two opposite things about Hinduism. First, they will say that Hinduism is a recent construct, a colonialist legacy that emerged only over the last 200–300 years (which may be partially true, but the idea of a common dharmic approach is millennia old). In short, there was no Hinduism before the British colonized India, with foreign 'Orientalists' creating a new Hindu consciousness that resulted from their own understanding of how religions get defined in the Christian context. In the Left-secularist view, there is no such thing as Hinduism, since diversity and local difference were what defined people living in India for centuries. Hinduism is created only in opposition to Hindutva.

By this logic, all Hindu subgroups should be considered minorities in independent India, since there is no overarching identity called 'Hindu.' But the secular Left brigade will also argue that Hindus have an overwhelming majority in India, and because of that, Hinduism is a threat to minorities. If Hindus are disparate groups with no common identity, how did they suddenly become a mythical majority?

There are two lessons for Hindus who do not want to either join the fringe or become self-loathing Hindus themselves.

First, they must study their adversaries and adopt tactics and strategy based on local, national and global conditions for the spread of Indic ideas. This means they have to become proselytizing faiths themselves. A new, improved ghar wapsi product is needed. But even more important is the export of Indian faiths to the West, where the market is ripe for its growth. Hinduism is a good option for people looking to move beyond the base camp of narrow dogma. Buddhism could, for example, be the religion of peace and enlightenment to export to West Asia, Europe and the Americas. Jainism may be the right religion to promote with the growing band of 'veganists' and animal rights activists. I am not just being facetious here.

Second, they must master the language of sophistication and modernity. Islam and Christianity became 'universal' faiths by massacring and coercing their enemies and demonizing the 'other'. In the twenty-first century, this is not an option for any religion, including a more self-confident Hinduism that sees value in the past even while embracing new ideas. The problem is we want to see greatness only in our past, whereas it lies in what we do now.

The right way to look at our past is with pride, but with the future in focus. We have to tell ourselves: 'We are proud of what we achieved in the past. But will our ancestors be proud of what we are doing now?' The past is over; Hindus have the world to conquer by looking at the future.

13

HOW THE SYSTEM WORKS AGAINST HINDU INTERESTS

Before we talk about the creation of a dharmic state, or at least about moving towards that concept of nationhood, one question needs asking: what is wrong with 'secularism', or *panth nirpekshata* (neutrality between religions), which is the core principle enshrined in our constitution? Why should Hindus, or the dharmic religions, seek special protection for their interests and religious rights?

The answer is this: in India, secularism has come to mean special protections to minorities and debasement of Hindu rights. This was not what the Constitution intended when it inserted Article 25 on the freedom of conscience and the subsequent Articles (26, 29 and 30, in particular) sought to assure the minorities that their rights are safe in India. But for Hindus, it is the exact reverse that has happened. The state, the politicians and the courts have taken Articles 25, 26, 29 and 30 to mean that Hindu rights need no protection and can do with some debasement. Thus, nearly 100,000 temples remain under state control in five southern states (despite court judgments to the contrary). Personal laws are 'progressive' for the dharmic religions, but the minorities have their own special laws, and there are special minority commissions and ministries catering to the exclusive interests of minorities. The Right to Education Act, 2009, which burdens private schools to educate the poor, specifically excludes unaided minority institutions from its ambit. And so on.

Worse, 'secular India' can never speak for Hindu minorities anywhere, in the neighbourhood or elsewhere. The Citizenship (Amendment) Act, 2019, which was intended to fast-track citizenship to minorities from Pakistan, Bangladesh and Afghanistan who have been persecuted by Islamist regimes, was instantly converted into a campaign about Muslim exclusion in India, though no rights of existing citizens were targeted. A film, *The Kashmir Files* (2022), which highlights the ethnic cleansing and targeted killings of Kashmiri Pandits in 1990, was attacked for being anti-Muslim. *Time* magazine called it a 'further descent into bigotry'.[1] A Qatar-based media house, Aljazeera, talked of 'the dangerous truth of *The Kashmir Files*'.[2] The CNN fretted about India's 'deepening religious divides'.[3]

What articulate and reasonable Hindus are demanding is not primacy but equal rights and the right to express concerns over the human rights of fellow Hindus. But this is apparently not acceptable to secular and minority intellectuals.

In 2019, after a small group of Hindus met in Delhi to script demands for 'equal rights', Faizan Mustafa, vice-chancellor of Nalsar Law University, Hyderabad, wrote an article in *The Tribune*, Chandigarh, rubbishing the idea of equal rights. He wrote:

> It sounds bizarre that at a time when the Hindu nationalist party has Hindutva as its main plank, and 303 seats in the

> Lok Sabha and governments in most states, Hindus feel so insecure that they want rights that the Constitution has given to the minorities. One must salute this leadership for instilling fear in the majority community, despite 80 per cent share in population and total domination of the power structure. The BJP has been talking of 'justice for all and appeasement of none' in opposing minority rights. Decades ago, a BJP panel under KR Malkani had proposed the deletion of Article 30 that gives minorities the right to establish and administer educational institutions of their choice. Today, there is a demand to give minority rights to Hindus as well.[4]

It is odd that someone associated with a law university should have a problem with 'equal rights'. But as Thomas Sowell, an African-American economist and intellectual, put it pithily on Twitter, 'Civil rights used to be about treating everyone the same. But today some people are so used to special treatment that equal treatment is considered to be discrimination.'[5] This is exactly the problem with secularism in India. It privileges minority rights over equal rights, and the idea that minorities must have special rights is hardcoded into the Constitution, and political and judicial thinking.

The fact that we supposedly have a 'majoritarian' and 'Hindu nationalist' government at the Centre and some states has made no difference to the idea that minorities must be given special privileges. In March 2017, Satya Pal Singh, a BJP minister in Modi's ministry in his first term, proposed a private member's Bill to ensure equal rights by suggesting amendments to articles in the Constitution that gave special rights only to minorities.[6] Among the four major amendments he proposed were:

(1) A proposal to repeal the 93rd constitutional amendment, which allowed only minority institutions to be exempt from the Right to Education Act. Singh's Bill wanted to remove Clause 5 of Article 15, which was added to exempt only minority-aided or unaided institutions from the Right to Education Act. Clause 5 reads:

> (5) Nothing in this article or in sub-clause (g) of clause (1) of article 19 shall prevent the state from making any special provision, by law, for the advancement of any socially and educationally backward classes of citizens or for the Scheduled Castes or the Scheduled Tribes in so far as such special provisions relate to their admission to educational institutions including private educational institutions, whether aided or unaided by the state, other than the minority educational institutions referred to in clause (1) of article 30.

Three other clauses that Singh's bill wanted to insert were the following:

(2) Notwithstanding anything contained in article 25, the state shall not control, administer or manage, whatsoever, any institution, including its properties, established or maintained for religious or charitable purposes by a religious denomination or any section thereof.

(3) All laws in force in the territory of India in so far as they are inconsistent with the provisions of this article shall, to the extent of such inconsistency, be void.

(4) The state shall not make any law which enables it to control, administer or manage, whatsoever, any institution, including its properties, established or maintained for religious or charitable purposes by a

> religious denomination or any section thereof, and, any law made in contravention of this clause shall, to the extent of such contravention, be void.

That a bill to ensure equal rights has almost no political support even in the BJP shows how secularism, in the way it has been implemented in India, has essentially worked against Hindu interests. Article 25 (1) states that 'all persons are equally entitled to freedom of conscience and the right freely to profess, practise and propagate religion'.

Can Hindus 'propagate' their religion when the primary means of doing so and the control of religious institutions are often in the hands of the state, especially in southern India?

In the Sree Padmanabhaswamy, temple case, the Supreme Court gave a final verdict—after 11 years of judicial ruminations at various levels—in favour of retaining the traditional trusteeship of the Travancore royals, but not without adding many riders.[7]

First, it shifted the trusteeship back to the Travancore royals, as was the tradition ever since the mid-eighteenth century, when Marthanda Varma transferred his kingdom to the presiding deity, Padmanabhaswamy, and declared himself his *dasa*, or servant of the deity, in whose name the kingdom would henceforth be ruled. The Supreme Court order in 2020 agreed that the mere abolition of princely titles cannot end the terms under which Travancore signed up to the Indian Union (the ruler signed the instrument of accession in his capacity as Padmanabha Dasa [Servant of Padmanabha], and not as the actual ruler). But when it restored the trusteeship to the royals, it also imposed a shift in the power structure in favour of the state.

Second, a five-member administrative committee was

set up, which would be headed by the Thiruvananthapuram district judge and two nominees from the Kerala and Union governments. Only the head priest and the royal family nominee were the real stakeholders in the temple, with two votes in five.

Third, the judgment, delivered on 13 July 2020 by a bench with U.U. Lalit and Indu Malhotra as members, imposed tough conditions on the temple management. Among them, it shifted the cost of providing security to the management of this temple, which was said to house treasures worth over ₹100,000 crore, when its formal earnings were barely ₹1.5 crore monthly. At the time of judgment, it was not in a position even to pay salaries to employees.[8] The judgment stated: 'It must also be stated that the present security arrangements as deployed by the State Government shall be continued, but the expenses in that behalf shall be borne by the Temple hereafter'.[9]

Fourth, the judgment ordered a 25-year audit of the temple. It asked the new advisory committee, to be headed by a retired high court judge, to 'order audit for the last 25 years, as suggested by the learnt *Amicus Curiae*. The audit shall be conducted by a firm of reputed Chartered Accountants'.[10]

Such long-term audits have never been ordered even on scam-tainted promoters or companies, but a temple is supposed to do so. Needless to say, the audit will take years to complete, and during that time, the temple managers will be constantly looking over their shoulders for what surprise the accountants may spring on them. Temple freedom, even when grudgingly granted, comes with plenty of strings attached.

On the other hand, the higher judiciary tends to go out of its way to protect minority interests, both directly and indirectly.

Here is just an example, mentioned briefly earlier. In October 2021, the Madras High Court decided that SC certificates cannot be denied to anyone even though they now adopt Christian symbols at work or at home after marrying a Christian.

The judgment, according to a *Times of India* report, noted:

> There is no suggestion in the affidavit that she has abandoned her faith or that she has embraced Christianity. It is equally possible that she, as a part of a family, may accompany her husband and children for Sunday *matins*, but the *mere fact that a person goes to church* [emphasis added] does not mean that such person has altogether abandoned the original faith to which such person was born.[11]

This judgment makes it near impossible, without intrusive invasions of privacy, to establish anyone as Christian even after conversion.

Two factors work against Hindu interests in secularism, Indian style, especially when it pertains to judicial interventions. First, there is Article 25, which guarantees 'freedom of conscience and free profession, practice and propagation of religion' but inserts an exclusion only for Hindus, by allowing the state to intervene while '(b) providing for social welfare and reform or the throwing open of Hindu religious institutions of a public character to all classes and sections of Hindus'. Clause 2(a) allows the state to intervene in the secular activities of religious institutions (see below).

So, any judge can use this clause to insert the state into issues involving Hindu faith, as the Sabarimala verdict of 2018 did. The five-judge bench threw open the doors of Swami Ayyappa to women in the reproductive age (barred due to the celibate nature of the deity being worshipped as a *naisthika bahmachari* in this shrine). Justice D.Y. Chandrachud said this exclusion was akin to the practice of 'untouchability'.

The use of clauses 2(a) and (b) is worsened by the judiciary's unwillingness to read Hinduism on the latter's own cultural ground, making Hindu rights fair game for judicial interventions.

In December 2021, the Supreme Court directed the Andhra Pradesh government not to bar non-Hindus from participating in auctions for shops or malls under the Charitable and Hindu Religious Institutions and Endowments Act, 1987.

In Tamil Nadu, a college established under the Tamil Nadu Hindu Religious and Charitable Endowments Act, was—at the time of writing—facing a challenge in the Madras High Court for restricting the recruitments to Hindus only. The challenge is by a Muslim.[12]

Both cases should have been thrown out on arrival, for Hindu devotees are not obliged to bankroll jobs or business ventures of non-Hindus within the premises of institutions funded by their contributions. But the higher judiciary clearly may not think so. This indicates that the judiciary, informed as it is only by narrow constitutional issues, is doing damage to Hindus by additionally being culturally insensitive or ignorant.

This cultural illiteracy and anti-Hindu bias have been in play after the country tilted leftwards in the 1960s, and both judges and academic institutions favoured covert anti-Hindu stances.

Two issues in particular involve cultural illiteracy and/or intellectual bias. The first is the distinction being made between religious and secular activities in Hindu institutions.

While earlier Supreme Court judgments, especially those given before the country's politics turned leftwards in the 1960s, tended to agree that there is no clear way to separate religious from secular activities in temples, later judgments, including one in the Andhra Pradesh case, have tended to go with the idea that these two can indeed be separated. This mischief is the direct result of the Christian idea of secularism, which involves the separation of church and state, the spiritual from the temporal, born out of the European Christian historical experience of conflict between the two institutions.

In India, such tensions have been rare, except under Muslim rule. Indian kings, even if their personal beliefs were Buddhist or Jain, have contributed generously to Hindu temples, Shaivite kings to Vaishnavite temples, and vice versa. The idea of kings being benevolent towards all faiths is intrinsic to Indian thought, and there was seldom any need to separate the spiritual from the temporal with regards to the point of view of the state. The Chanakyan mantra, '*Sukhasya moolam dharmah, dharmasya moolam arthah*', clearly suggests that dharma cannot be divorced from economics and wealth.

Pavan K. Varma, in his book *The Great Hindu Civilisation*, notes the same thing: that kings and emperors may follow their own faiths, but they often donated money to other faiths, which were seen as part of the same family, though different. Thus, Emperor Ashoka was said to be Buddhist, but most of the caves carved out during this time in Barahar (Bihar) and in the time of his grandson were those of the Ajivika sect. He adds:

> The Bharhut stupa railings, originally in central India, brings us for the first time specific Buddhist themes,

> including Jataka stories. These were made under the rule of Sunga kings, who personally worshipped Hindu deities... In the first century CE, under the rule of the Satavahana kings, great entrance gateways were made to the large stupa at Sanchi. These continued Buddhist themes. Inscriptions show that the Satavahana rulers followed Hindu deities and were fully generous to the Buddhist sangha.[13]

If there is no clear way to separate purely religious activity from the non-religious parts, the decision that Hindu religious institutions must have a separate track for inducting non-Hindus to benefit from secular activities is violative of the constitutional spirit of allowing each religion the freedom to manage its own affairs.

Counterfactually, even if one can indeed separate religious from secular functions in a temple, common sense should have informed the judiciary that once non-Hindus are installed inside a Hindu institution, there is nothing to prevent them from clandestinely or openly spreading their own religious ideas. Will the courts, for example, intervene to stop a Christian shop-owner from distributing pamphlets for church services nearby when he can claim that Article 25 gives him the right to propagate his religion? One cannot presume that the highest courts will not uphold such absurdities in the future, given its past track record. And if Muslim show-owners decide to offer namaz on the premises of a Hindu institution, one presumes that cannot be stopped either in the name of freedom to practise one's religion. If Hindus object, they can be pilloried for being intolerant.

Secondly, the real damage may be coming from two constitutional provisions: Article 25(2) and Article 26.

Article 25, which guarantees 'freedom of conscience and free profession, practice and propagation of religion' adds in its second and third provisos.

> (2) Nothing in this article shall affect the operation of any existing law or prevent the State from making any law...(a) regulating or restricting any economic, financial, political or other secular activity which may be associated with religious practice; (b) [providing] for social welfare and reform or the throwing open of Hindu religious institutions of a public character to all classes and sections of Hindus.

Article 26 guarantees citizens the freedom 'to every religious denomination or any section thereof [...] (a) to establish and maintain institutions for religious and charitable purposes; (b) to manage its own affairs in matters of religion; (c) to own and acquire movable and immovable property; and (d) to administer such property in accordance with law.'

Since Articles 25(2)(a) and (b) allow the state to regulate 'any economic, financial, political or other secular activity which may be associated with religious practice', in the case of Hindu institutions, this gives the state a licence to not just regulate but also control them. That around 100,000 temples in five southern states are directly under state control does not appear to have bothered either the secular state or the super-secular judiciary. The right to regulate has become the right to total control by the state.

Article 26, which should provide comfort to every Hindu sampradaya, has, in fact, been used specifically to deny Hindus the autonomy given to Christian and Muslim religious institutions since Indian temples belonging to specific sampradayas do not fit the Christian meaning of the word 'denomination'. In theory, sampradaya should have been seen as the equivalent of denomination for legal purposes, even though the two words convey radically different meanings, but that hasn't always been the case.

The five-judge bench that decided the Sabarimala case simply refused to see the issue as one involving a denomination's rights, or that the celibate deity, Swami Ayyappa, had any rights at all. The basic Hindu idea of viewing the deity as a living entity after prana prathistha is simply ignored by the judiciary. In short, the sheer usage of western or Christian theological terms to define Hindu institutions, compounded by the cultural illiteracy of the higher judiciary, has been used to deny Hindus their core rights.

The next time the judiciary takes up Hindu issues, Hindu petitioners should insist that they be assisted in their interpretations of Hindu rights under the law with the help of true practitioners from various sampradayas. Judicial cultural illiteracy, or an unwillingness to acknowledge Hindu cultural sensitivities and rights while interpreting the law, needs addressing.

14

RAM JANMABHOOMI, KASHI, MATHURA AND DEITY RIGHTS

It is interesting to note that in the Ram Janmabhoomi judgment delivered by a five-judge bench headed by the then Chief Justice of India Ranjan Gogoi on 9 November 2019, which included justices Sharad Bobde, Ashok Bhushan, S. Abdul Nazeer and D.Y. Chandrachud, the primary argumentative pivot used by the bench to award the site fully to the Hindus was by treating the dispute as one about property and not faith.

The judgment clearly stated:

> In the present case, this Court is tasked with an adjudicatory task of unique dimension. The dispute is over immovable property. The court does not decide title on the basis of faith or belief but on the basis of evidence. The law provides us with parameters as clear but as profound as ownership and possession. In deciding title to the disputed property, the court applies settled principles of evidence to adjudicate upon which party has established a claim to the immovable property.

> On the balance of probabilities, there is clear evidence to indicate that the worship by the Hindus in the outer courtyard continued unimpeded in spite of the setting up of a grill-brick wall in 1857. Their possession of the outer courtyard stands established together with the incidents attaching to their control over it.
>
> As regards the inner courtyard, there is evidence on a preponderance of probabilities to establish worship by the Hindus prior to the annexation of Oudh by the British in 1857. The Muslims have offered no evidence to indicate that they were in exclusive possession of the inner structure prior to 1857 since the date of the construction in the sixteenth century. After the setting up of the grill-brick wall, the structure of the mosque continued to exist and there is evidence to indicate that namaz was offered within its precincts. The report of the Waqf Inspector of December 1949 indicates that Muslims were being obstructed in free and unimpeded access to mosque for the purposes of offering namaz.[1]

This, and the fact that an idol of Ram Lalla was installed in the 'intervening night of 22/23 December 1949', and the idols were allowed to be worshipped inside the mosque by the lower courts, helped the Hindu claims. The Supreme Court, despite tut-tutting at this 'desecration' of a mosque, which was subsequently brought down by *kar sevak*s (volunteers for religious service) on 6 December 1992, effectively used the argument of adverse possession to award the site finally to Hindus.

On the other hand, the bench did reaffirm that the deity '*Bhagwan Shri Ram Virajman*', and his birthplace (the Ram Janmabhoomi), were juridical entities. The bench, even while dismissing Hindu claims to Ram Janmabhoomi based on faith, upheld another suit, filed by a 'next friend' on behalf of the deity in 1989, as maintainable.[2]

In another judgment, in 1994, the Supreme Court held that the mosque was not central to the practice of Islam. The case pertained to the acquisition of 67 acres of land around the Babri Masjid in 1993 by the P.V. Narasimha Rao government under the Acquisition of Certain Area at Ayodhya Act, 1993, which was challenged by a Muslim, Dr Ismail Faruqui. The petitioner claimed that a mosque is central to the practice of his faith, and hence its acquisition by the state is illegal.

The judgment rejected this claim on common sense grounds, saying that: 'A mosque is not an essential part of the practice of the religion of Islam and Namaz (prayer) by Muslims can be offered anywhere, even in open. Accordingly, its acquisition is not prohibited by the provisions in the Constitution of India.'[3]

This should have been obvious since even airports today have prayer rooms for Muslims, which can't be called mosques, and namaz is sometimes allowed even on public roads, for special occasions, in several states, much to the consternation of residents in crowded localities. Public roads, too, cannot be called the equivalent of mosques, which are an important part of Islam, but they are not the only places where Muslims can offer namaz.

In 2018, another three-judge bench headed by then Chief Justice of India Dipak Misra, declined to reopen the judgment in the Faruqui case.[4] Three points are worth mentioning here.

One, the judiciary can be counted upon to do the right thing but often based on arguable premises. The Ayodhya judgment went in favour of Hindus but without establishing faith as an important element in the judgment.

Two, the disputes over the Hindu holy places of Kashi (Varanasi) and Mathura, where, too, during the reign of Aurangzeb, a mosque and an *idgah* were built on the site of demolished temples, cannot be adjudicated on the same basis as Ram Janmabhoomi (that is, adverse possession by Hindus), since Hindus do not have possession of the mosque and idgah areas. What they have is faith and historical evidence, which has been sought to be sidelined by the Places of Worship (Special Provisions) Act, 1991, which was enacted *before* the Babri structure was demolished. The Act prevented any changes in the ownership of places of worship after 15 August 1947. To make their case, Hindus have to circumvent both the Ayodhya judgment, based on adverse possession, and the Places of Worship Act.

Three, a key element that will be important to decide Kashi and Mathura is the issue of deity rights. The Ayodhya judgment accepted the deity as a juristic person, but a future judgment will have to go further and accept the deity as a real person in the eyes of devotees, one with constitutional rights. In short, the deity or murti is not just a piece of clay, wood, metal or stone, but a real person under the law. In the context of the growing movement for freeing Hindu temples from government control—an outrageous imposition on followers of Hinduism's various sampradayas—the issue of deity rights cannot be brushed under the carpet.

But first, let us get some common objections out of the way. If you are a social justice warrior or someone with rationalist inclinations, you are entitled to ask: how can a murti, whether made of clay, stone or metal, and admittedly sculpted by human beings, be given the same rights as living, breathing human beings?

The answer is simple. Let us first understand that a murti

is not the same as what our westernized minds call an 'idol'. Murti puja is not idol worship. After it is consecrated, a murti is invested with *prana* (life) by priests on behalf of devotees through the *prana pratishtha* (establishment of prana) ceremony. This point aside, let us raise two other questions.

One, do only human beings have 'rights' outside the world of spirituality? The answer is a clear no, for in the judicial world, a non-natural person—whether a corporation or any other legal entity—is also considered a 'juristic person', who can own property, be a party to a dispute, pay taxes, etc. In the US, the Supreme Court, in *Citizens United Versus Federal Election Commission*, held that free speech rights exist even for non-natural persons like corporate bodies or their funded agents.[5] So, yes, rights exist for deities even if you do not consider them to be 'persons' in the commonly understood sense of the term. The only question is: what kind of rights do they have?

Two, has the deity been accorded person status in the past? Again, the answer is yes, which even the Supreme Court acknowledged in the Ayodhya case. Even when India was ruled by the British, the law accorded the Hindu deity the status of a minor with rights, with priests and other temple managers only acting as trustees of the minor. This point was established as far back as in 1869, the year of Gandhi's birth, in a case involving *Maharani Shibessourie vs Mothooranath* Acharjo, where the British Privy Council held that the *shebait* (the manager of the deity) was only a trustee acting on behalf of the deity. The trustee had no ownership rights of his own. This principle was reiterated in the Dakor Temple case of 1887, where the Bombay High Court held that the 'Hindu idol is a juridical subject and the pious idea that it embodies is given the status of a legal person'.[6] In later cases, the deity was said to have rights to receive gifts and hold property, among other things. The simple point is that a deity may have trustees to manage temporal affairs but has rights of its own.

The issue has come back into public consciousness for two reasons.

One is the Sabarimala case, where a five-judge constitutional bench ruled 4:1 that women in the reproductive age cannot be barred from entering the sanctum sanctorum just because Lord Ayyappa is worshiped as a naisthika brahmachari. J. Sai Deepak, one of the lawyers arguing the case, said that Lord Ayyappa had his own rights as a deity, which was dismissed out of hand: 'Merely because a Deity has been granted limited rights as juristic person under statutory law does not mean that the Deity necessarily has constitutional rights.'[7]

This is debatable, for the Constitution is a human document which can be changed and has, in fact, been repeatedly changed in 70-plus years of constitutional history. Nothing stops a government or a court from treating this as another basic structure issue in a country where deities are worshipped in such large numbers.

Interestingly, the Supreme Court gave more than just juristic status to the Guru Granth Sahib, the Sikh holy book. In a case involving the *Shriomani Gurdwara Prabandhak Committee vs Shri Som Nath Dass and Others on 29 March, 2000*, the apex court said that the 'Guru Granth Sahib [...] cannot be equated with other sacred books... Guru Granth Sahib is revered like a Guru... [and] is the very heart and spirit of [the] gurudwara. The reverence of Guru Granth, on the one hand, and other sacred books, on the other hand, is based on different conceptual faith, belief and application.'[8] It was the tenth Guru, Guru Gobind Singh, the last of the Sikh gurus, who declared that after him the Guru Granth Sahib would be the ultimate and eternal guru for Sikhs. The court, of course, emphasized that the Guru Granth Sahib 'cannot be a juristic person unless it takes juristic role through its installation in a gurudwara or at such other recognised public place'.[9]

This logic should equally apply to any Hindu deity installed inside a temple after due consecration and prana pratishtha, which is the act of infusing the murti with prana (life/breath), making it a living entity in the eyes of its devotees. If the courts can recognize a holy book as a living guru, and deities anyway are considered minors with rights, what is the basis for denying the deity its own individuality and constitutional rights?

The logic here is: what is worshipped and how depends on devotees, and if the deity worshipped is seen as the equivalent of a living entity, then that is how it should be.

The Supreme Court lost an opportunity to pronounce in favour of deity rights in the Sree Padmanabhaswamy Temple case, where the erstwhile rulers of the state of Travancore had a special relationship with this temple of Vishnu in Thiruvananthapuram, the modern-day capital of Kerala.

In 1749, the then ruler of Travancore, Marthanda Varma, took the momentous decision of declaring Lord Padmanabha the actual ruler of the state and relegated himself to being his dasa, taking decisions in the Lord's name. From then on, all rulers called themselves Padmanabha Dasas and this continued even after the state acceded to the Indian Union after 1947. This linkage between the descendants of Marthanda Varma and the temple remained alive till the courts again entered the picture after allegations of mismanagement were hurled.

In a judgment delivered on 13 July 2020, where the descendants of Varma were the main appellants, Justices

U.U. Lalit and Indu Malhotra refused to go into the special relationship between the rulers and descendants of Marthanda Varma and their special relationship with the deity. Instead, the bench merely ruled that Varma's descendants would be the nominal shebaits or trustees of the temple, aided by two committees—one advisory and another administrative.

While the Sree Padmanabhaswamy judgment does not restore deity rights, it does open up avenues for erstwhile rulers of princely states, who were often the shebaits of various temples, to consider whether they, too, can return to their traditional roles as managers and benefactors of major temples. The Mysore Royals, for example, have been shebaits to the Mysore Sri Chamundeshwari Temple and some others, often built with private funds.

One reason why the Sree Padmanabhaswamy case went partially in favour of the descendants of Varma was that the accession of the princely state to the Indian Union was itself done with Lord Padmanabhaswamy as ruler. The king acted in his capacity as the Lord's dasa and representative. In short, the 'Cochin State Instrument of Accession and Standstill Agreement signed between Kerala Varma, Ruler of Cochin State and the Dominion of India' was signed by Shri Chithira Thirunal Balarama Varma as a representative of the deity in whose name the state had been ruled for 200 years before accession.

Common sense informs us that deities are critical to Hindu forms of puja. During Islamic rule, when temples were being demolished by bigoted rulers in pursuit of their own iconoclastic inclinations, devotees and priests made it a point to smuggle out the deity to a safe place when the temple itself could not be saved from destruction. Thus, even more than the temple, the deity was the life being protected. This fact has been noted in historian Meenakshi Jain's book, *Flight of Deities and Rebirth of Temples*.[10]

Today, with the Sabarimala judgment providing a wake-up call to all devotees, the fight for deity rights is being led by, among others, Sri Chilkur Rangarajan, the hereditary priest of the Chilkur Balaji temple in Telangana. However, his plea before a nine-judge constitutional bench looking to review the Sabarimala judgment was rejected in 2021, which has subsequently led to a shift in focus from the courts to the executive. The nine-judge bench anyway has to be reconstituted now that many of the appointees have retired.

Letters have been written by not only Sri Chilkur Rangarajan but also by the descendants of Krishna Deva Raya (who took the Vijayanagar Empire to its crest of glory in early sixteenth century), the Raja of Jatprole, S.V.K.B. Adithya Lakshma Rao and the BJP MP from Bengaluru South, Tejasvi Surya. All of them have supported deity rights and sought the intervention of the president and the prime minister to confirm the rights of Lord Padmanabhaswamy and, in the process, extend the idea to all deities.

The fight for the return of temples to devotee-led institutions, as opposed to the state running them, will be incomplete without the restoration of deity rights. After all, the deity belongs to devotees, and devotee rights are inseparable from that of the deity.

15

SMALL GAINS, BIG CHALLENGES IN 'FREE TEMPLES' MOVEMENT

The Supreme Court verdict of 13 July 2020 in the Sree Padmanabhaswamy temple case, which handed back control to its erstwhile trustees—the descendants of the Travancore-Cochin royal family—gives us a vantage point from which to evaluate the progress made by the 'Free Hindu Temples' movement among Hindus.

The movement—which includes everyone from lawyers dedicated to the cause of dharma to organizations such as the Vishwa Hindu Parishad, and individual politicians such as BJP Rajya Sabha MP Subramanian Swamy—can roughly be said to have three broad objectives: one is to get Left historians and the general public to acknowledge the damage done by erstwhile Islamic rulers, who destroyed thousands of temples in their bigoted, iconoclastic zeal, and restore them to Hindu ownership, either to rebuild or to build afresh (Ayodhya Ram temple, Kashi, Mathura, etc).

The second prong of the movement is to retrieve the damage done under British colonial rule, where Hindu temples—and Hindu temples alone—were brought under state control. This continues even after Independence, especially in southern India. It is estimated that over 100,000 temples are under state control in five southern states.

The third prong is preventive, even defensive: the idea is to stop further state ingress into temple management. The Sree Padmanabhaswamy temple case and the Uttarakhand government's bid to impose state control on Char Dham temples (plus 51 more), through the Uttarakhand Char Dham Devasthanam Management Board Act, 2019, fall in this category. The Bill has since bitten the dust after strong protests from the temples' traditional priesthood, but that is another story. The attempt to expand state control of Hindu temples has not ended. Even in the Ayodhya Ram temple, while the Supreme Court verdict restored the site to Hindus, it mandated a role for the government in this transition. At some point, the temple's management should be separated from the government. But it is early days on that front, given the importance attached by the BJP to the building of the Ayodhya temple before the 2024 Lok Sabha elections.

There are thus battles being waged on three primary fronts: retrieval of temples destroyed or built over by Muslim rulers in the past; retrieval of Hindu temples already under state control, especially in the southern states, and prevention of further takeovers of temples by states. A fourth battle, which has been clubbed by the Supreme Court along with issues relating to other religions, is Sabarimala in Kerala and Shani Shingnapur in Maharashtra. It involves the rights of temples to follow their own traditional rules and practices.

Before we discuss this further, here is a synopsis of the state of the war to regain control of temples by civil society and devotees.

1. Reclamation of temples erased or built over by Islamic rulers in pre-colonial India. The first major victory is the Supreme Court verdict of November 2019 in the Ram Janmabhoomi case, where a five-judge bench headed by the then Chief Justice of India Ranjan Gogoi voted 5-0 to hand the property to Hindus and asked the state to give Muslims a five-acre plot of land as compensation to build a mosque elsewhere. But there are two flies in the ointment: one, even before the Babri structure was demolished, the Narasimha Rao government, obviously in a bid to balance the 'secular' image of the Congress, passed the Places of Worship (Special Provisions) Act, 1991, which disallows Hindus from reclaiming—even through courts—the desecrated or demolished Kashi and Mathura temples.[1] This left only Ayodhya as a disputed site. Till this law is repealed, there is a legal impediment to Hindus claiming their destroyed temples, or the sites of built-over temples. The second problematic issue with the Ram Janmabhoomi verdict is that it again brings the state into the picture in managing temples. The Ram temple trust, called the Shri Ram Janmbhoomi Teerth Kshetra, has been formed by the Centre under court orders, and includes many genuine Hindu stakeholders. But it leaves behind a ticklish issue of separating state from temple management open once more.

2. The second challenge is to retrieve temples from government control. This is proving to be long-winded, since no state government is willing to let go of temples even after many judgments in favour of Hindus. In January 2014, in what was truly a landmark judgment, a bench comprising justices B.S. Chauhan and J. Chelameswar, both now retired, asked the Tamil Nadu government to return the Chidambaram Natarajar temple to its original trustees, the

Podhu Dikshitars. The court held that:

> Even if the management of a temple is taken over to remedy an 'evil', the management must be handed over to the person concerned immediately after the 'evil' stands remedied. Continuation thereafter would be tantamount to usurpation of their proprietary rights or violation of the fundamental rights guaranteed by the Constitution in favour of the persons deprived. Therefore, taking over of the management in such circumstances must be for a limited period.[2]

This was a major victory, and the temple has since been handed back to the Podhu Dikshitars. But here's the problem: the court verdict should have forced the Tamil Nadu government's Hindu Religious and Charitable Endowments (HR&CE) department to consider framing laws to hand over the other remaining temples back to devotee control or non-state stakeholders, but that has not happened. And Tamil Nadu alone had 44,121 temples under the HR&CE ministry as in mid-July 2020.

According to T.R. Ramesh, a redoubtable warrior in the cause of freeing temples from state control and the president of the Indic Collective Trust, a non-profit outfit with similar objectives, the Tamil Nadu government's order releasing the Chidambaram Natarajar temple from HR&CE control talked only about this one temple. 'There are over 35,000 temples under TNHR&CE which earn less than Rs 10,000 monthly, but even these have not been released from government control.'[3]

Ramesh suggests that the only way out may be to file for a writ of mandamus in the Supreme Court directing state governments that the operative parts of the Chidambaram temple judgment should be extended to all temples. He files many court cases to prevent Tamil Nadu from encroaching further into temple management and/or restrain current custodians from allowing temple assets—whether land or ancient idols—to be frittered or stolen. But it is an uphill battle.

3. The third prong is prevention of state entry into temples that are already privately run. This is where the Sree Padmanabhaswamy case becomes relevant. In a verdict on 13 July 2020, a two-judge Supreme Court bench with Justices U.U. Lalit and Indu Malhotra—the latter being the lone dissenting judge in the 4-1 Sabarimala verdict which allowed women in the reproductive age to enter—said that control of the temple will revert to the descendants of the Travancore royal family, as was agreed to by the Indian government at the time this princely state was integrated into the Indian Union. As part of the agreed covenant, the control of the temple was to remain with the ruler of Travancore-Cochin even after the state acceded to the Indian Union. But in 1971, Mrs Gandhi abolished hereditary titles and privy purses by the 26th Amendment to the Constitution of India, thus leaving the gates open for a legal challenge on whether trusteeship rights for the temple could be passed on once there was no 'ruler' left to govern it. No one, including the state, challenged the rights of the last ruler of Travancore, Sree Chithira Tirunal Balarama Varma, who died in 1991, or that of his younger brother, Uthradom Thirunal Marthanda Varma, who stepped up to the same role after him. It was only in 2009, when a tenant (an advocate) was asked to vacate temple-owned premises, that court cases started getting filed challenging the rights of the successors to the former ruler of Travancore in managing the temple.

The Kerala High Court, in a judgment in 2011, rejected the rights of the royal family to manage the temple and said the state must step in.[4]

The state was also directed to audit the valuables and properties of the temple and display some of those in an exhibition centre within the temple complex. Control and day-to-day administration of the temple thus went from an executive officer appointed by the royal family to a state-appointed committee.

It is this that the Supreme Court has overturned to return trusteeship and overall control back to the royal family, but with caveats that the royal family itself proposed: a five-member administrative committee and a three-member advisory committee, both under the guidance of the royal family.[5] The administrative committee shall include one nominee of the ruling family, the chief *tanthri* (head priest), the district judge of Thiruvananthapuram (who shall be its chairman), and one nominee each from the Kerala government and the culture ministry at the Centre. The advisory committee will be headed by a former high court judge nominated by the Chief Justice of the Kerala High Court, a chartered accountant and a nominee of the royal family.

Viewed purely in terms of voting strength, two of the three members of the advisory committee and three out of the five in the administrative committee are representatives of either the judiciary or the state. This may pose no problem in the near future, since the immediate impact of the verdict will be seen to favour a return to the status quo as existed before 2009. But in the long run, one cannot be sure if politics and possible disagreements in the royal family itself may lead to any issues with the governance of the temple.

The Supreme Court verdict, which asks the temple to

bear the costs of its own security in future—now rendered more expensive after public discussion of its untold wealth has increased security risks—may need modification if the temple's revenues fall short of expenses, and some of its properties and assets need either rental rates revised or even sold.

The net gains from the Supreme Court verdict in the Sree Padmanabhaswamy judgment are the following: a) status quo has been restored and control shifted back to the royal family and two committees set up under his tutelage; b) the 'free Hindu temples' movement has now found effective legal advocates for its cause, and this will be vital for the future, as more battles need to be fought; and c) the Supreme Court, in handing over Sree Padmanabhaswamy to the erstwhile ruler of Travancore state, left a constitutional question mark over whether the deity had a special place in the scheme of things. After all, the Travancore-Cochin Maharaja signed the Instrument of Accession to the Indian Union in the name of Sree Padmanabhaswamy.

The reasons to worry are the following: a) it has taken nine years to reverse an illegality to restore authority back to the royal family; as long as the courts take so long to deliver verdicts, it means any troublemaker seeking to put a spoke in the wheels of the temple's administration can find a way to drag matters to court again; b) restoring the status quo depended heavily on the covenant signed between the ruler of Travancore-Cochin and the newly independent Government of India when the state acceded to India in 1949. This means, the decision may not be quoted as a precedent to free other temples from control, which do not have such special protections and covenants; and c) question marks remain over how the wealth and properties of the temple will be protected and, if necessary, monetized in future if costs soar. The possibility of a return to state meddling cannot be ruled out if there are dissensions within the royal family, or the heirs run out, or either the state or central government nominees decide not to play fair and create controversies over the decisions of the ruling family.

4. The battle to stop state interference in Hindu temple practices and rituals is still open. In Sabarimala, where Lord Ayyappa is worshipped as a naishtika brahmachari, woke feminists managed to get the Supreme Court to treat this as an unfair discrimination case even though other Ayyappa temples allow all to enter. The court also held that Sabarimala was not entitled to the protections of Article 26, which allow all religious denominations and their subsections to maintain their age-old practices. The Sree Padmanabhaswamy judgment explicitly side-stepped the Article 26 issue.

While a constitutional bench will finally decide this matter, it has gotten clubbed with practices considered questionable in other religions (mosque entry ban on women and female genital mutilation, among others). Apples and oranges will be judged together. But while there is still hope for Sabarimala, in the smaller Shani Shingnapur, a Maharashtra temple where women were not allowed into the sanctum sanctorum till 2016, the temple management, under pressure from a BJP-led state government, simply surrendered to feminist activism. The problem is that parties like the BJP and the RSS have shown little interest in deeper temple-related control issues.

The Uttarakhand Char Dham takeover, the Sabarimala judgment and the Shani Shingnapur cases show that the 'Hindu nationalist' party that many consider as 'guardian' of the idea of Hindu Rashtra may not have any special interest in freeing temples. Perhaps they don't see too many votes in taking up this issue.

This is the real fight that Hindus face: a 'secular' consensus against community control of temples. The BJP seems as 'secular' as the rest, especially when one notes its non-action on returning temples to devotee control and making changes to Articles 25 to 30, as mentioned earlier. By sheer inaction, it is indirectly aiding the expansionary interests of the Abrahamic religions—Christianity and Islam—for the latter's places of worship and the assets they generate can be funnelled back into proselytization. Hindus have to fight with their backs to the wall on two fronts: against the inert 'guardians' of Hindu interests, the BJP–Sangh Parivar, and against the conversion merchants of Islam and Christianity.

16

THE ROADBLOCKS TO EQUAL RIGHTS FOR HINDUS

Equal rights for Hindus in religious affairs face two roadblocks: one is the judiciary, which is not only reluctant to take up issues of importance to Hindu rights but is often unsympathetic to them; and the second is the 'secular-Left-liberal' ecosystem in academia and the mainstream media, which is focussed more on alleged 'majoritarianism' in India and in near-complete denial of Hindu concerns and issues.

Let's take the judiciary first. Nearly four years after the Sabarimala judgment, and at the time of writing this around the end of 2022, the Supreme Court had not even gotten down to setting up a constitutional bench to review that judgment. Nearly a decade after Swami Dayananda Saraswati, through writ petition 476/2012 (he has since passed away) challenged the legitimacy of the Hindu Religious and Charitable Endowments Acts of Tamil Nadu, Andhra Pradesh (before bifurcation) and Puducherry, which give the state control of thousands of Hindu temples, there is simply no forward movement on this matter. Nearly 67 years after the Shirur Mutt verdict, where a seven-judge bench headed by Justice B.K. Mukerjea said the state could not intervene in religious affairs, but sought to make a distinction between 'essential religious practices' and the secular activities of religious institutions, the anachronism of only Hindu temples being run by states remains.[1]

Ronojoy Sen, a former editor with *The Times of India* and senior research fellow at the Institute of South Asian Studies, National University of Singapore, critiques the Supreme Court's tendency to play arbiter in Hindu affairs, in a paper published in 2010: 'American courts have usually tried to avoid sitting in judgment on "religious error" or "religious truth". The Indian Supreme Court has travelled an opposite path, seeking to cleanse Hinduism of what it reads as superstition and providing it with a modernist and rationalist definition of religious error and religious truth.'[2]

In his paper, Sen has examined how 'the courts have attempted to define religion with respect to the Constitution, and second, how the (apex) court, in adjudicating cases related to Hinduism has drawn a distinction between the sacred and the secular'. He further noted that 'the most striking aspect of the essential practices doctrine is the attempt by the Court to fashion religion in the way a modern state would like it to be rather than accept religion as represented by its practitioners'.

This was most apparent in the Sabarimala judgment of September 2018, which has been discussed earlier.

In his paper, Sen quotes a withering comment by two eminent jurists, Rajeev Dhavan and Fali Nariman, on how the courts have taken it upon themselves to play high priests, using constitutional provisions under Articles 25, 15 and 17 as the weapons choice.

However, adding to this judicial tendency to play high priests while deciding Hindu religious cases, there is also the need to play to the 'liberal' gallery, especially to audiences abroad.

In a speech in July 2021, Justice Chandrachud (now Chief Justice of India) told an Indo-US conference on legal relations that the Supreme Court should play the role of a 'counter-majoritarian institution', and it was its duty to protect socio-economic minorities.[3]

This argument is seriously flawed for two reasons. One, the term 'majoritarian' is not relevant to the Indian context, where Hindus are not organized under one church or agreed on one set of fundamental laws.

There is nothing majoritarian about Hinduism, which is a ground-up set of ideas that grew autonomously on this soil. You can be Hindu without having to subscribe to any set of 'fundamentals' or believing in one prophet or one Son of God. You can even junk the idea of God.

Hinduism has elements that we can call religion, but it is not a religion as defined by Abrahamic norms. So, one wonders where Justice Chandrachud got his idea that the Supreme Court needs to stand against majoritarianism in the Indian context.

Clearly, the secular-Left-liberal use of words born out of the European historical experience, including words like 'majoritarian', 'fundamentalism', 'Islamophobia' and 'fascism', cannot be used to describe Hindu (or Hindutva) assertiveness. If any attempt is made to rewrite history with a more Indic perspective, it is decried as 'saffronization'.

Words like 'communal' are being used as opposites of 'secular', when communal merely refers to something that relates to a community or group. The word 'secular'—separation of church from state—is irrelevant in the Indian context, where religious and other forms of pluralism have been part of the warp and weft of Indic civilization. We need pluralism, not secularism.

Varna and jati are two different things, but under western, Abrahamic ministrations, they have been reduced to one idea—caste. This is not to defend caste (varna-based) bigotry or oppression in any way, but just to point out the difference between using the outsider's terminology to view ourselves. We could perhaps have dealt with the inequities of caste better if we had reformed it in our own way, but then we missed that opportunity when we substantially copy-pasted a constitution using western models.

Similarly, when we rewrite our history and other textbooks to bring in more elements of our own historical experiences and achievements, the real word to use is not 'saffronization', but de-Abrahamization, or reducing Eurocentricity.

This brings us to the question: what is de-Abrahamization? Large parts of India have been ruled by two sets of ideologies: Islamic and British (i.e. informed by Christian experience) over the last 1,000 years. Both are Abrahamic forces, and their post-colonial counterparts in American and European academies are essentially using Eurocentric or Abrahamic lenses to view their former colonies. De-Abrahamization means using more Indic lenses to view our past and our present.

The Abrahamic ideology involves a mutually exclusive binary, where religion has to be defined by specific fundamentals, where only one idea can prevail at a time (my god, not yours; my truth, not yours), and where 'science' is used to deny the possibility of truths being discovered by intuitive and introspective methods—which has often been the Indian way of discovering better truths.

Even though all truths finally have to be validated empirically, it does not mean that a truth cannot be subjectively realized and explained with reasonable coherence before we find the proof for it. Only a Eurocentric or Abrahamic mind could have invented a phrase like 'post-truth', as if truth itself has finally been established beyond all doubt, and all else is post-truth.

Our history has been written by 'Orientalists'—to use Edward Said's term—who have largely used western lenses to view the past and explain the present, and our Left-liberals (often illiberals) have appropriated the same colonial lenses.

The Marxist interpretation of history, based on materialism, is a valid way of looking at history, but it is clearly not the *only* way to do so. Human history is not shaped by material drives alone. And Indian history, in particular, has been driven by other motivations, including spirituality, high intellectualism and a sense of the sacred.

What Marxist history has done is a typically Abrahamic thing: relabelled all other interpretations of history as wrong, or 'communal', or written by the wrong people. The irony, that all recent Indian history has been written only by such Left-liberal and western think tanks has been lost on these ideologues.

India needs to create its own strong Indology departments run by people with an Indic sensibility. At the same time, we need to look at the Occident with our lenses—just as they view us with theirs.

At some point, it would be fine if someone in the West complains about Indians using Indic lenses to define the West and Islamic nations, but then, they are free to write their own version of Orientalism, and call it Occidentalism.

Right now, we are still under the grip of western Orientalism and Indology. The immediate need is to detoxify Indian history and rewrite it by de-Abrahamizing or de-Orientalizing it. Saffronization is not the issue here. At least, not yet.

The second, and more objectionable point made by Justice Chandrachud in his 2021 speech is the suggestion that the court must tilt in one direction, in favour of 'socioeconomic minorities'. This is no different from Dr Manmohan Singh saying that the first right on state resources must be the minorities.[4]

In theory, one need not object to helping those who are in a minority and unable to defend their interests, but underlying this is the assumption that if you are not a 'socioeconomic minority', your claims to justice are secondary to the primary focus of the highest court.

If this is not about tilting the balance against people designated a non-minority, what is? Is this why the Supreme Court has almost never tried to conclusively address the issues relating to equal rights for Hindus?

There are some judges who are loved by India's Lutyens media and Left-liberals, but it seems that they are planning to introduce their own ideas of what constitutes justice, using their own lenses, and those of legal luminaries in the West.

Earlier this year, in a case involving giving women permanent commissions in the army, Justice Chandrachud rightly said that women and men cannot be judged by the same set of seemingly objective criteria. But instead of merely acknowledging that women and men are built differently and hence 'inclusion' should mean using different criteria for women (as happens in sports, etc.), Justice Chandrachud chose to rely on arguments in a British case.[5]

In 2009, Baroness Hale of the United Kingdom Supreme Court held that 'direct and indirect discrimination are mutually exclusive. You cannot have both at once. The main difference is the direct discrimination cannot be justified. Indirect discrimination can be justified if it is a proportionate means of achieving a legitimate aim'.[6]

Did the court need a UK judgment to bolster his case for giving women equal rights to obtain a permanent commission in the army by choosing criteria that is relevant to them? Why use some obscure judgment from our colonial masters to justify a simple issue of deciding on inclusion without using such intellectually empty arguments? Can courts really act against all forms of indirect discrimination when most humans are not born equal and have different abilities?

The idea of inclusion does not need support from the idea of 'indirect discrimination' to work. Now, everybody can claim indirect discrimination based on unequal outcomes resulting from any set of standards.

The Supreme Court was also involved in overturning the Sabarimala temple's rule that expects women in the reproductive ages to stay out till they turn 50. Swami Ayyappa is worshipped as a naisthika brahmachari, a celibate, in this unique temple. Instead, the judgment brought in the concept of 'untouchability' to rule that the temple's practices were discriminatory.

The issue in Sabarimala was never about untouchability, for it bars only women in a specific age group. Not all Swami Ayyappa temples have this norm, and this unique temple did not deserve the judiciary's prejudicial use of the term 'untouchability' to let women of all ages enter the shrine.

The problem with such woke liberalism is that it is writing its own death sentence. Liberalism was good as long as its purpose was to protect the individual against the vagaries of older institutions like family, tribe, religion, race, etc.

But now that this objective has largely been achieved,

liberalism is likely to lose traction as it has turned the individual into an enemy of the society at large.

The balance between individual rights and collective community interests, where rights are balanced with responsibilities to the larger society we are part of, is making the state larger and larger than ever at the cost of community.

In the name of protecting individual human rights, liberalism has dug its own grave by destroying the community on which the individual depends for making social life meaningful. Man is a social animal, and his individuality has to have some respect for the larger interests of society. And vice versa.

I could have said that liberalism has lit its own funeral pyre and not dug its grave, but this virulent form of liberalism that some judges seem to represent is a purely western import. Yes, it has dug its own grave.

Which brings me to the next point: the subtle Hinduphobia of the 'secular-Left-liberal' elite in India. The Left has been particularly Hinduphobic, and nothing demonstrates this better than how it tried to mangle history to its own ends.

The autobiography of a former regional director of the Archaeological Survey of India, K.K. Muhammed, shreds the last fig-leaf of legitimacy from India's 'eminent' leftist historians, and even the broader Indian Left ecosystem, which includes most mainstream political parties and large sections of the old media in print and TV. (*Eminent Historians: Their Technology, Their Line, Their Fraud* is the title of a book by Arun Shourie, which establishes the biases of our leftist historians.)[7]

In his book titled *Njan Enna Bharatiyan* (I, An Indian), published in 2015–16, Muhammed indicts Left historians for actually *preventing* a rapprochement between Hindus and Muslims over the building of a Ram temple in Ayodhya. The Left historians made the Muslim side adopt intransigent positions. *Firstpost* quotes him as saying this:

> The Babri issue would have been settled long ago if the Muslim intelligentsia had not fallen prey to the brain washing by the Leftist historians. A set of historians, including Romila Thapar, Bipin Chandra and S. Gopal argued that there was no mention of the dismantling of the temple before [the] 19th century and Ayodhya is a Buddhist-Jain centre. They were supported by historians Irfan Habib, R.S. Sharma, D.N. Jha, Suraj Bhan and Akthar Ali.[8]

Weeks after the book's publication, mainstream media was not keen to discuss this beyond quoting the usual suspects about Muhammed's lack of understanding of historiography. This tells us how the ecosystem can kill truths that are self-evident to any normal individual.

Suppressio veri, suggestio falsi (Suppress the truth, suggest falsity) is the norm, as Shourie pointed out in his brilliant critique of leftist historiography in *Eminent Historians.*

Muhammed's assertion that the Left historians actually scuttled efforts at a compromise is buttressed by the fact that even after the Allahabad High Court judgment of 2010, which tried to create one more opportunity for compromise between the two communities by apportioning two-thirds of the disputed area to Hindu groups and one-third to Muslims, the Left historians criticized the judgment as a travesty.[9]

As a non-Left historian, Meenakshi Jain notes in her book *Rama and Ayodhya*, the leftist critique of the Hindu demand for a temple in Ayodhya kept shifting arguments depending on how much of their lies got proven wrong at any point of time. She writes:

> Initially, they [the Left historians] asserted that the disputed structure [the Babri Masjid] was constructed on a spot that was neither a place of worship, nor the site of any previous Hindu religious structure, nor was there any evidence to associate it with the birthplace of Rama. However, as the ASI excavations [ordered by the court] progressed, 'a marked change' in their approach became evident. Some archaeologists appearing on behalf of the Sunni Wakf Board tried to 'set up a new case' that there appeared to be an Islamic structure below the DS [disputed structure].[10]

And when the excavations showed not one but several pillars of a Hindu temple at the Babri site, the argument again changed to bring in a new element: that Ayodhya was known as a place for Buddhist–Jain influence. This was a transparent effort to muddy the waters by trying to bring in a new element of conflict to make the previous conflict unresolvable.

There is only word for such sophistry: dishonesty. There is only politics, no historiography and very little historical rigour in the Left's assertions on behalf of the Muslim side of the argument. The only logical—and sensible—argument to make against the Babri verdict was a simple one: whatever be the Islamic history of the destruction of Hindu temples, demolishing a mosque that now stood on a temple site is wrong because today's Indian Muslims had no role to play in the destruction of the temple that stood on the Babri site. But instead, they went to absurd lengths to prove what was manifestly untrue.

We have been very indulgent with the Left and its efforts to play around with the truth because we implicitly believed two things about them: that they have their hearts in the right place, as they care for the less fortunate. And, more importantly, they had no stake in casteism or communalism, since their basic issue was class warfare.

However, the reality is otherwise.

As the Sachar Committee report showed, the condition of Muslims in West Bengal after more than a quarter century of leftist rule was among the worst in the country.[11] The Left's alleged empathy for the disadvantaged is more about theory, little about practice.

As for the other assumption—that it has no stake in communalism—Muhammed's assertion that they actively tried to scuttle a settlement between Hindus and Muslims shows that Left historians were working to promote communal trouble.

The Left routinely accuses the BJP and the Sangh of fascism but has nothing to say about its multi-decade admiration for two acknowledged mass murderers in history apart from Hitler: Stalin and Mao. It is time for all of us to sit and exclaim: The Left has no clothes.

If leftist historians have any shame, they should apologize to the nation for their past dishonesties, whether it is in writing dubious history or in how they have defended the indefensible.

However, that may be expecting too much from people who think dishonesty is fine in their pursuit of class warfare. It is written in their holy book, written by one Karl Marx.

17

A RETURN TO DHARMA FOR ALL INDIANS

The assumption that if India becomes a Hindu Rashtra, or dharmic nation, it will reduce Indian Christians and Muslims to second-class citizens is a fear that needs addressing. Yes, it cannot be business as usual, but it does not imply any negative impact on the rights of Christians and Muslims to be full citizens of Bharat and practise their faiths without restrictions.

The main constraints Islam and Christianity will face in a dharmic nation will be twofold: one is a restraint, preferably accepted voluntarily, on aggressive proselytization without in any way deterring any individual's desire to change his or her religion. There will be no constraints on the practices and traditions of either of the two Abrahamic religions.

The second constraint will be the challenge to existing mindsets. Both Christianity and Islam are conceived as ever-expanding faiths, with the ultimate goal being to bring all humans under one universal faith (their own). This is nothing but imperialism in matters of faith, even though cultural pluralism exists in almost all faiths. It cannot foster true communal amity since the basic aim is to grow one's own faith at the cost of the others. Gandhi abhorred conversions for a simple reason: it makes the whole of religion about numbers, which is politics by another name. At its very core, religion should be about a deepening of spirituality, so that we can all seek higher truths and deep insights into our place in the cosmos. While Gandhi was not opposed to voluntary conversions, he spoke out against conversions by the offer of inducements.

While Indian Christianity, especially the older and established churches, are not aggressive proselytizers or abusers of Hindus, the same cannot be said about some of the evangelical Protestant churches that are mushrooming all over South India and gradually spreading to the North. The latter gain converts by rubbishing Hinduism, even while many of them adopt Hindu symbols like the Dhwaja Sthamba (the flagpole near the entrance of many southern temples) that are now ubiquitous in many churches but with a Cross on top. Many churches use dharmic terminology to spread the message (terms like 'jyoti', 'gyan', 'sadhna', 'puja', etc. are now in wide use in many churches and denominations). These churches will scream blue murder when curbs are placed on their use of any and all means to convert Hindus and others.

However, they must ask themselves a simple question: when they have had the advantage of huge resources and millennia of practice to convert themselves into proselytizing organizations, which Hinduism has not had, isn't it only fair that Hindus get time to catch up by building their own proselytizing institutions? Don't we place handicaps on the forward castes who have had huge starting advantages over the SCs and STs to level the field for the latter? Hindus are asking for time to bring their religious institutions to standards where they can hold their own against the churches. The fact that over 100,000 temples are still under state control in five southern states of India tells us how hobbled Hindus are in a secular state.

A mindset change is required by Muslims in India, too, for several reasons. One is their historical memories of having been rulers in India, and as long as this thought remains, it will be difficult to live in peace, especially after Muslims demanded, and got, a separate state of their own in 1947.

However, the bigger challenge for Muslims in a dharmic nation is their own core dualistic approach to ethics, with one norm for Muslims and less favourable norms for non-Muslims.

As Ambedkar wrote in his tract on *Pakistan, or the Partition of India*:

> Hinduism is said to divide people and in contrast Islam is said to bind people together. This is only a half truth. For Islam divides as inexorably as it binds. Islam is a close corporation and the distinction that it makes between Muslims and non-Muslims is a very real, very positive and very alienating distinction. The brotherhood of Islam is not the universal brotherhood of man. It is brotherhood of Muslims for Muslims only. There is a fraternity, but its benefit is confined to those within that corporation. For those who are outside the corporation, there is nothing but contempt and enmity.[1]

Ambedkar also fretted about whether Islam can live in peace within a modern nation.

> The second defect of Islam is that it is a system of social self-government and is incompatible with local self-government, because the allegiance of a Muslim

> does not rest on his domicile in the country which is his but on the faith to which he belongs. To the Muslim *ibi bene ibi patria* is unthinkable. Wherever there is the rule of Islam, there is his own country. In other words, Islam can never allow a true Muslim to adopt India as his motherland and regard a Hindu as his kith and kin. That is probably the reason why Maulana Mahomed Ali, a great Indian but a true Muslim, preferred to be buried in Jerusalem rather than in India.[2]

Bill Warner, who has written several books on Islam and noted this dualistic approach to ethics, has this to say about the religion.

> Islam divides the entire world into Islam and kafirs and has two sets of ethics, one for Islam and another for the rest. The Golden Rule has the equality of all humanity as its basis. It is not: Do unto *some* people, as you would have them do unto you, but do unto *all* people as you would have them do unto you.
>
> Islam denies the universality of the Golden Rule because Islam starts with the division of the entire world, all humanity, into two different groups—Islamic and non-Islamic. Every aspect of Islamic ethics is based upon this separation. Having two distinct groups leads to two different ethical codes. Said another way, Islam has dualistic ethics.[3]

Ram Madhav, a senior member of the RSS and former national general secretary of the BJP, said in an interview to an online publication that Muslims would face no problems in following the five core pillars of their religion, but they would have to tone down three other things: the concept of ummah, kafir and jihad.

He said:

> Islam has five pillars—loyalty to the religion, *namaz* five times a day, *zakat* or donation for the welfare of the people, fasting during Ramadan and taking a pilgrimage to Mecca or Medina. Follow that, nobody will stop you (the Muslims) in this country. There are three other things that come in the way of the large issue of inclusivity in national society.
>
> The concept of ummah means 'we are a separate nation, because we are Muslims'. They have to give this up. They have to stop believing in the whole concept of *kafir*. According to them, non-Muslims are *kafir*, or sinners. In day-to-day parlance, nobody is a *kafir*. They have to stop using that [term]. And then they have to sacrifice their way of jihad. If it is jihad, it has to be internal. Many Muslim scholars say 'jihad has to be internal.' Jihad does not mean you kill people of other religions.[4]

To this, one can add one more thing: a willingness to accept a single common civil code for all Indians.

The idea of a dharmic nation poses no threat to the practice of Christianity and Islam, but it invites them to adjust their core concepts, which were developed in Europe and West Asia, respectively, in their formative years, to Indian cultural sensibilities. In Bharat, exclusivity in matters of faith and belief do not add up to 'freedom of religion'. It is about a bifurcation of humanity into 'us and them'.

In contrast, Savarkar, a man much vilified for his tract on Hindutva, comes closest to defining Hindu Rashtra as not a religious entity, but a cultural one. He wrote:

> Ever since the Vedic ages, our forefathers had been shaping the formation of our people into a religious, racial, cultural and political unit. As a consequence of it all, growing organically, the Sindhus of the Vedic time have grown today into [the] Hindu Nation, extending over India and holding India in common as their fatherland and their Holy Land. No other nation, excepting perhaps the Chinese, can claim a continuity of life and growth so unbroken as our Hindu Nation does [...] It has grown out of this soil and has its roots struck deep and wide in it. It is not a fiction invented to spite the Muslims or anybody in the world.[5]

As journalist Uday Mahurkar and Chirayu Pandit write in their book, *Veer Savarkar: The Man Who Could Have Prevented Partition*, 'Savarkar's Hindutva is culturally Hindu but its effect is secular',[6] for it does not intend to discriminate against those Indians who changed their faith to Islam or Christianity in the past, for whatever reason.

Some modern Muslims, despite believing (mistakenly) that a Hindu Rashtra will be majoritarian and theocratic in construct, do accept that a redefinition of India need not be negative. Hasan Suroor, an Indian Muslim author settled in Britain, wrote in a recent blog on *The Times of India* website that the idea of a Hindu Rashtra need not be discriminatory against the minorities:

> A state can have an officially recognised religion—in India's case, it will be Hinduism—and yet remain secular in practice by treating all citizens as equal and making sure that their religious and civil rights are protected by law—as in many western liberal democracies, including

> Britain, where the state is Christian, but government practices are secular.[7]

In India, it will work even better, for the very idea of being Hindu means accepting plurality and diversity as a given. But, of course, will our 'secular-liberals' agree? The biggest roadblocks to equal rights are self-appointed defenders of minorities.

The larger question is: will evangelical Christianity have an easier time adjusting to the notion of a dharmic nation? My personal intuition is that they will, since they have already been strong in including Indic elements into Christianity, as I mentioned earlier, but the real problem relates not to the religion but how Christianity secularizes itself.

In the West, true believers in Christ as the only agent of redemption are dwindling in number. Surveys by Probe Ministries and the Pew Research Center show that a majority of even born-again Christians believe in pluralist traditions, and no longer believe that only Jesus is the way to heaven.

The *Christian Post*, quoting a survey by Probe Ministries, reports that 'nearly 70% of born-again Christians disagree with the biblical position that Jesus is the only way to God [...] The survey, which looked at religious beliefs and attitudes toward cultural behaviours, polled 3,106 Americans ages 18 to 55 from all religious groups, including 717 respondents who identified as born-again Christians'.[8]

Pew Research, in a 2018 survey, noted that though 'most American adults self-identify as Christians', many 'also hold what are sometimes characterised as "New Age" beliefs—including belief in reincarnation, astrology, psychics and the presence of spiritual energy in physical objects like mountains or trees. Many Americans who are religiously unaffiliated also have these beliefs'.[9]

Another Pew Research Center report has this to say:

> In popular culture, meditation often is associated with Eastern spirituality and its secular offshoots, such as mindfulness. But substantial shares of Americans of nearly all religious groups—as well as those who have no religious affiliation at all—say they meditate at least once a week. Americans tend to say they meditate regularly (40% do so at least weekly) or rarely, if at all (45% seldom or never do). There's not much middle ground—only 8% say they meditate once or twice a month and only 4% say they do so several times a year.[10]

This brings us to an interesting point. S.N. Balagangadhara, who has spent a lifetime studying the science of cultures, says that one way Christianity sometimes expands is by secularizing itself, i.e. by de-Christianizing itself.[11]

One manifestation, possibly, of de-Christianized Christianity is liberalism, or wokeism, which is its current avatar. Wokeism is defined in neutral terms by a Wikipedia entry as 'alert to racial prejudice and discrimination'.

The Urban Dictionary is less charitable, and defines it as 'the state of an individual being so "self-aware" and "socially aware" that they become completely oblivious to the issue, intention, or objective at hand'. Thus, being liberal should mean being tolerant, but if you are a woke liberal, you cannot even allow a non-woke conservative to express their opinion. It's cancel culture.

The biggest mindset change will actually have to be made by Hindus themselves, for they have allowed themselves to be conned into the belief that what they inherited from the past is not worth much. Worse, there is hope that since dharmic ideas (in some form or the other) have survived for five millennia, they need no special efforts to retain their freshness in the future. Just as environmental damage needs human corrective action on a global basis, protecting dharma in the land of its birth needs concerted action.

Ambedkar exhorted the SCs to 'educate, agitate, organize' to claim their rightful place in India and elsewhere. This is what Hindus must do over the current and next generation or two.

In the Mahabharata, as also in the *Manu-smriti*, there is an all-powerful message: *Dharmo Rakshati Rakshitah.* That is, 'Dharma protects those who protect dharma'.

This is as true for Hindus, as for Muslims and Christians in India, who must see the protection of dharma, which is not religion in this context, but the plurality of the universe, and acceptance of difference as the primary truth in life, as central to their own survival.

Evidence from contemporary history tells us that whenever plurality dies, there is more warfare, not less. After two world wars, Europe entered a third intra-European war between Russia and Ukraine. The Muslim world is more divided against itself than against the rest of the world, as we are seeing in the whole of West Asia and in Pakistan. The so-called liberals are at war with liberalism. Wokeism is killing common sense liberalism. In India, dharma will protect Islam and Christianity as long as they respect and protect dharma.

In one line, whether it is Christianity, Islam, communism or woke liberalism, they need to moderate themselves to be in conformity with dharmic balance. That is the only way India can be at peace with itself, despite its diversity and plurality.

The question is: can anyone impose a dharmic mindset upon those unwilling to accept it? The answer is no. But one can make a beginning in some non-coercive ways. The third way is by legislating more effective laws to crimp the foreign funding lifelines of the conversion merchants.

A few ideas that may help are the following.

One, given past history of animosity between Hindus and Muslims, historical memories can be whittled down by creating a permanent History, Truth and Reconciliation Commission, where historical wrongs are acknowledged and put behind. This way Muslims can move on, as they no longer have to carry the burden of what their forefathers or rulers may have done to harm Hindus.

Two, communities—whether Hindus and Muslims, or upper castes and Dalits—should negotiate their own agreements for peace through a give-and-take process, where both sides know what they have gained for what they have given up. Where such agreements are worked out, they should be given the force of law. The rule of law works best when communities think it is in their interest to agree on them, not as something imposed from above. The rule of law should reinforce what communities have negotiated among themselves.

Three, all Indian adults, and anyone who becomes Indian by naturalization, should be asked to swear an oath of allegiance to India, that is Bharat. In the US, naturalized citizens are required to take this oath, with some leeway given to atheists. The oath runs thus:

> I hereby declare, on oath, that I absolutely and entirely renounce and abjure all allegiance and fidelity to any foreign prince, potentate, state, or sovereignty, of whom or which I have heretofore been a subject or citizen; that I will support and defend the Constitution and laws of the United States of America against all enemies,

> foreign and domestic; that I will bear true faith and allegiance to the same; that I will bear arms on behalf of the United States when required by the law; that I will perform non-combatant service in the Armed Forces of the United States when required by the law; that I will perform work of national importance under civilian direction when required by the law; and that I take this obligation freely, without any mental reservation or purpose of evasion; so help me God.

An Indian oath of allegiance can be reworked around this core idea. We can delete or add some phrases, which can include not only defending and upholding the Constitution but also dharma, and a willingness to respect all religions without exception.

It could read something like this:

> I, Shri/Smt/----------------- do swear that I will be faithful and bear true allegiance to India, that is Bharat, and to the Constitution of India as by law established, that I will uphold the sovereignty and integrity of India, and that I will carry out my duties as a citizen in the largest interest of preserving dharma. I owe no loyalty to any power or country outside this sacred land called Bharat.
>
> I acknowledge that India, that is Bharat, is a multi-faith country, and as such all faiths are equal and worthy of respect. I hereby promise to respect all Indian faiths as equal and on a par with my own faith. I will not seek to actively convert or participate in religious activities where the objective is to convert people from other faiths to my own faith, for I acknowledge that all faiths have their own validity in their approach to

> higher truths. I additionally accept that even those who do not believe in God or religion deserve my respect and acceptance.
>
> I also acknowledge that I can be stripped of my citizenship in case I am found to be wanting in upholding this oath, whether through active subversion or indirect support to others who do not believe in upholding the multi-faith, syncretic character of India. Dharma is indivisible, and so are the people of India.

Words like 'kafir' should be banned or outlawed just as calling Dalits by their caste names is legally treated as abuse.

Fourth, non-dharmic religions, such as Christianity and Islam, should consciously become dharmic in nature even while worshipping their own gods. Individuals in these faiths should, as a first option, consider returning to dharma from which they were violently parted in the past, but even if they choose to retain their current faith, they need to change their approaches to them. They have to abandon the exclusivity and imperialistic implications of their faith. And yes, they should consider making amends for the past, when the torchbearers of their faith looted and degraded Bharat for their own narrow ends. Just as Nazi Germany was asked to compensate the victims of Nazism, these faiths should consider compensating dharmics not with any money or wealth but by restoring what they unlawfully and unfairly took over—the temples at Kashi and Mathura, for example. The best form of compensation, however, is not monetary or material but returning to dharmic principles.

At some point, once we obtain a period of living together without rancour, the dharmic spirit will seep into most Indians, no matter what their religious beliefs. What cannot work is to have predatory religions living in close contact with non-predatory, non-proselytizing religions. Someone has got to lose in this situation, and the loser will surely become desperate at some point and turn violent.

In one line, the two should meet at midpoint. It means Hindus must harden their sense of identity and become more of a proselytizing religion, while Christians and Muslims must soften theirs and focus on inner spiritual growth to unite with their dharmic brethren. This way we can create a new kind of Bharat that draws on its 5,000-year-old heritage and improves on it.

Dharmo Rakshati Rakshitah. Dharma protects those who protect India's dharmic nationhood. The countdown for India's dharma-based Second Republic has begun.

ACKNOWLEDGEMENTS

In many ways, this book was written in instalments. The work for it truly began towards the end of 2015, when I moved away from mainstream media so as to be able to write more freely on the issues I cared about, and which I could not manage to do when writing for the 'secular' media. The primary debt I owe is to *Swarajya* magazine, which provided me with a platform to develop my thoughts on Hindu and dharmic issues on a daily basis and write about them. When I joined *Swarajya* in 2015, thanks to an unexpected invitation from Hari Kiran Vadlamani, writing a book was farthest from my mind. It was only in 2021, when I started writing long-form articles for the magazine's website, that I saw the potential for writing a book in phases. The magazine's two co-founders, Prasanna Viswanathan and Amar Govindarajan, who were closely involved with the conception and production of the magazine, need particular mention as people who encouraged and supported my long-form pieces, which form an important part of this book. A website usually does not like long-form articles, for readers tend not to have the kind of patience when reading from laptops or hand-held devices. Some 80 per cent of this book was published in *Swarajya*.

Towards the second half of 2021, Dibakar Ghosh of Rupa contacted me to consider the possibility of writing a book.

I quickly agreed, only to discover my folly later. I found the whole process of using existing materials and writing new stuff to make the whole book coherent driving me crazy. And—I must confess now—it was only Dibakar's persistence and patient coaxing that convinced me to continue even though I was ready to give up at many points. I cannot but thank him, and Manali Das, who painstakingly edited the book, profusely for their support and help. And last, of course, I have to mention my wife, who had to put up with my book-writing tantrums without too many protests.

But, most important, I cannot but pay my deep respects to the scores of dharmic and Hindu intellectuals who have made it easier for me to understand the nature of the challenges we face, and how to meet them. In particular, I must mention the early influence of writers like Ram Swarup, Sita Ram Goel, Arun Shourie, Koenraad Elst and C. Rajagopalachari (Rajaji), in this context. Rajaji, who wrote two wonderful books on the Ramayana and the Mahabharata, was coincidentally associated with the founding of *Swarajya* itself. These intellectuals showed me the return route from deracinated secularism to dharmic reality. I cannot even begin to thank the countless other writers who wrote books to aid the dharmic cause, over the last two decades. To all of them my heartfelt pranams.

NOTES

INTRODUCTION

1 Varna is the four-fold layering of society defined by broad vocations, while jati is more of a cohesive group of people and not limited to the varna system.

2 Jagannathan, R., 'How Abrahamics Imprisoned and Debased the Idea of God and Religion', *Swarajya*, 23 October 2021, https://bit.ly/3g8Zhxf, accessed on 17 October 2022.

3 Swarup, Ram, 'Doctrinal Affinity, But Historical Conflict', *Hindu View of Christianity and Islam*, Voice of India, Delhi, 2011, pp. 21–22.

4 Henley, Jon, 'Sweden's Failed Integration Creates "Parallel Societies", Says PM After Riots', *The Guardian*, 28 April 2022, https://bit.ly/3D4ze3d, accessed on 17 October 2022.

5 'Merkel Says Germany Has "No-Go" Areas, Govt Won't Say Where', AP News, 28 February 2018, https://bit.ly/3MHsiw7, accessed on 18 October 2022.

6 Traynor, Ian, 'Swiss Vote to Ban Construction of Minarets on Mosques', *The Guardian*, 29 November 2009, https://bit.ly/3eANs2C, accessed on 18 October 2022.

CHAPTER 1

1 Balagangadhara, S.N., and Sarika Rao, *What Does It Mean To Be 'Indian'?* Notion Press, 2021, p. 19.

2 'Hindu Countries 2022', World Population Review, 2022, https://bit.ly/3T8e9uk, accessed on 18 October 2022.

3 'Global Christianity – A Report on the Size and Distribution of the

World's Christian Population', Pew Research Center, 19 December 2011, https://pewrsr.ch/3S3VM8J, accessed on 18 October 2022.

4 'Muslim Majority Countries 2022', World Population Review, https://bit.ly/3D6bhZx, accessed on 18 October 2022.

5 'The Global Religious Landscape: Hindus', 18 December 2012, Pew Research Center, https://pewrsr.ch/3UcqSMF, accessed on 1 November 2022.

6 '16 Nations Condemn Remarks on Prophet Mohammed as Blowback against India Spreads', NDTV, 7 June 2022, https://bit.ly/3Vvps1v, accessed on 18 October 2022.

7 Subramanya, Rupa, 'Crying Wolf: The Narrative of the Delhi Church Attacks Flies in the Face of Facts', *Firstpost*, 17 February 2015, https://bit.ly/3S4XTJb, accessed on 18 October 2022.

8 'Minute by the Hon'ble T.B. Macaulay, dated the 2nd February 1835', https://bit.ly/3zbHZ9B, accessed on 18 October 2022.

9 'The British Rule in India: Karl Marx in the New-York Herald Tribune 1853', *New-York Herald Tribune*, 10 June 1853, https://bit.ly/3MGddLp, accessed on 18 October 2022.

10 Jain, Ayesha, '"Dismantling Global Hindutva": Branded Hinduphobic, Academic Seminar Sparks Row', *The Quint,* 10 September 2022, accessed on 31 October 2022.

11 Jagannathan, R., 'Western Academia Progresses from Hinduphobia to Hindumisia—Hindu Hatred', *Swarajya*, 16 August 2021, https://bit.ly/3VBEsur, accessed on 18 October 2022.

12 Truschke, Audrey, *Aurangzeb: The Man and the Myth,* Penguin Random House India, Gurgaon, 2017.

13 'The Scholar Whom Audrey Truschke Cites Finds Her Tweets Shocking', *Swarajya*, 24 April 2018, https://bit.ly/2CVfQHs, accessed on 18 October 2022.

14 Truschke, Audrey, 'The Living Mahabharata', *Aeon*, 6 November 2020, https://bit.ly/3gilSrn, accessed on 18 October 2022.

15 'Rashmi Samant Resigns as Oxford Student Union President-Elect after Row over Her Past Remarks', *The Indian Express*, 18 February 2021, https://bit.ly/3D6PXTA, accessed on 18 October 2022.

16 'Petition Demands Oxford Apologise for "Hinduphobic" Staff Member amidst Investigation', *The Oxford Student*, 28 March 2021, https://bit.ly/3SaTchh, accessed on 18 October 2022.

17 Ibid.

18 Filmer, Antonia, 'Findings of Oxford Probe into Samant's Complaint Still Confidential', *Sunday Guardian*, 24 July 2021, https://bit.ly/3ggX3vE, accessed on 18 October 2022.

19 Chari, Mridula, 'A University in US Rejects $3 Million Donation from a Group with Hindutva Links', *Scroll.in*, 22 February 2016, https://bit.ly/3eEft9j, accessed on 18 October 2022.

20 'Call for US Probe into Hindu Right-Wing Groups Getting COVID Fund', Aljazeera, 8 April 2022, https://bit.ly/3gXoZFt, accessed on 31 October 2022.

21 'Hindus for Human Rights & Indian American Muslim Council Leaders, Rutgers Professor Audrey Truschke Sued for Defamation and Conspiracy against HAF', HAF, 7 May 2021, https://bit.ly/3gfcZyC, accessed on 18 October 2022.

22 Sewa International, https://sewausa.org/About-Us, accessed on 18 October 2022.

23 Harlankar, Samar, 'Lynchistan: Hindus Silent as a Wave of Violence against Muslims Sweeps India', *Quartz India*, 25 June 2017, https://bit.ly/3TxsjFo, accessed on 18 October 2022.

24 Jagannathan, R., 'Shashi Tharoor's "Why I am a Hindu" Is Driven by a Degree of Schizophrenia', *Swarajya*, 20 February 2018, https://bit.ly/3D6uxGc, accessed on 18 October 2022.

25 Ibid.

26 Balagangadhara, S.N., and Sarika Rao, 'ET's Hipkapi & Europe's Hinduism', *What Does It Mean to Be 'Indian'?* Notion Press, 2021, p. 123.

27 Ibid. 24.

28 Sharda, Ratan, and Yashwant Pathak, *Conflict Resolution: The RSS Way*, Garuda Prakashan, Gurugram, 2021, pp. xxvi–xxvii.

CHAPTER 2

1 Jagannathan, R. 'The Real Challenge of Defining Hindu Rashtra, from Ambedkar to Savarkar', *Swarajya*, 11 June 2020, https://bit.ly/3D50tdT, accessed on 18 October 2022.

2 Tharoor, Shashi, 'Shashi Tharoor: A Hindu Pakistan Would Not Be Hindu at All; It Would Be a Sanghi Hindutva State', *ThePrint*, 13 July 2018, https://bit.ly/3tAP2Fy, accessed on 16 November 2022.

3 Sanghvi, Vir, 'The Taste with Vir: What If India Had Become a Hindu Rashtra?' *Hindustan Times*, 5 June 2020, https://bit.ly/3D6xKWo, accessed on 18 October 2022.

4 Ibid.

5 Ambedkar, B.R., Chapter XIV, 'The Problem of Pakistan', Part VI, 'The Problems of Population Transfer Are Solvable and Need Not Detain Us', *Pakistan, or the Partition of India*, https://bit.ly/3EMdhHD, accessed on 18 October 2022.

6 Swamy, Subramanian, *The Ideology of India's Modern Right*, Har-Anand Publications Pvt. Ltd, 2018, p. 39.

7 Ibid. 35.

8 Ambedkar, B.R., Chapter II, 'A Nation Calling for a Home', Paragraph VII, *Pakistan, or the Partition of India*, https://bit.ly/3T65esN, accessed on 31 October 2022.

9 Ambedkar, B.R., *Pakistan, or the Partition of India*, Siddharth Books, Delhi, p. 137.

10 Ambedkar, B.R., Chapter VII, 'The Stand of Mr. V.D. Savarkar and the Hindu Maha Sabha', Part II, *Pakistan, or the Partition of India*, https://bit.ly/3D72SVA, accessed on 18 October 2022.

11 Renan, Ernest, 'What Is a Nation?' 1882, archived by Global Policy Forum (GPF), https://bit.ly/3D6EeVe, accessed on 18 October 2022.

CHAPTER 3

1 Ambedkar, B.R., *Riddles in Hinduism: The Annotated Critical Selection*, Navayana, 2016, p. 63.

2 Prabhu R.K., and U.R. Rao, 'My Hinduism Is Not Exclusive', *Mind of Mahatma Gandhi (Encyclopedia of Gandhi's Thoughts)*, Navajivan Mudranalaya, Ahemadabad, p. 318, https://bit.ly/3gfJcpI, accessed on 18 October 2022.

3 Swami Vivekananda, 'Swami Vivekananda's Speeches at the World's Parliament of Religions, Chicago, 1893', Belur Math, https://bit.ly/3SaLCmJ, accessed on 18 October 2022.

4 Radhakrishnan, S., *The Hindu View of Life, Upton Lectures Delivered at Manchester College Oxford 1926*, George Allen & Unwin Ltd, London and The Macmillan Company, New York, https://bit.ly/3TcCsav, accessed on 18 October 2022.

5 Golwalkar, Madhav Sadashiv, *We or Our Nationhood Defined*, Bharat Publications, Nagpur, 1939, p. 64, p. 77.
6 Savarkar, V.D., *Hindutva: Who Is a Hindu?* Hindi Sahitya Sadan, 2003.
7 Ibid. 114.
8 Mookerji, Radhakumud, 'The Hindu Institution of Pilgrimage and Its Significance', *Nationalism in Indian Culture*, Mysore University Extension Lectures, p. 33.
9 Eck, Diana L., Chapter 1, 'A Sacred Geography: An Imagined Landscape', *India: A Sacred Geography*, Harmony, Reprint edition (2013), p. 6.
10 Ibid. 116.
11 Sharda, Ratan, 'Inculcating Values and Sense of Nationhood through Festivals', *RSS 360: Demystifying Rashtriya Swayamsevak Sangh*, Bloomsbury, 2018, p. 115.
12 Ambedkar, B.R., Chapter VII, 'The Stand of Mr. V.D. Savarkar and the Hindu Maha Sabha', Part II, *Pakistan, or the Partition of India*, https://bit.ly/3Tf7MW7, accessed on 19 October 2022.
13 Ibid.
14 'Delhi Minority Commission Chief Says Hindus Will Face an Avalanche If Muslims Complain to Their Friends in the Arab World', *Opindia*, 29 April 2020, https://bit.ly/3VByvxQ, accessed on 18 October 2022.
15 Janmohamed, Zahir, 'US Evangelicals, Indian Expats, Teamed Up to Push Through Modi Visa Ban', *The New York Times*, 5 December 2013, https://nyti.ms/3gihUz0, accessed on 19 October 2022.
16 Golwalkar, Madhav, Sadashiv, *We or Our Nationhood Defined*, Bharat Publications, Nagpur, 1939.
17 'Golwalkar's "Bunch of Thoughts" Not Eternal, Says Bhagwat in RSS Outreach to Muslims', News18, 20 September 2018, https://bit.ly/3eHSvhC, accessed on 18 October 2022.
18 Jagannathan, R., 'Hindu Rashtra: From Golwalkar to Bhagwat, Evolution and "Neti-Neti"', *Swarajya*, 30 June 2020, https://bit.ly/3TxkT4R, accessed on 19 October 2022.

CHAPTER 4

1 'The Treaty of Westphalia', *History Today*, vol. 48, no. 10, 1998, https://bit.ly/3yVmOrZ, accessed on 19 October 2022.

2 Stepan, Alfred, et al., 'The Rise of "State-Nations"', *Journal of Democracy*, July 2010, https://bit.ly/3D6fOes, accessed on 19 October 2022.

3 J. Sai Deepak, 'Reclaiming a Civilisational Approach to the Constitution?' *The Daily Guardian*, 8 May 2020, https://bit.ly/3eIOIRe, accessed on 19 October 2022.

4 Swamy, Subramanian, *The Ideology of India's Modern Right*, Har-Anand Publications Pvt Ltd, 2018, p. 34.

5 Kakar, Sudhir, 'What Is Indian-Ness? By Forgetting Sympathy, India Is in Danger of Losing Its Highest Civilisational Ideal', *The Times of India*, 21 July 2019, https://bit.ly/2JHQrDP, accessed on 19 October 2022.

6 Ambedkar, B.R., Chapter XII, 'National Frustration', Part V, 'The Vision of Pakistan Is Powerful and Has Been Implicitly Present for Decades', *Pakistan, or the Partition of India*, https://bit.ly/2P7dA3X, accessed on 19 October 2022.

7 Ambedkar, B.R., Chapter X, 'Social Stagnation', Part I, *Pakistan, or the Partition of India*, https://bit.ly/3Wi2Cur, accessed on 31 October 2022.

8 Kakar, Sudhir, 'What Is Indian-Ness? By Forgetting Sympathy, India Is in Danger of Losing Its Highest Civilisational Ideal', *The Times of India*, 21 July 2019, https://bit.ly/2JHQrDP, accessed on 19 October 2022.

9 *Supreme Court Judgment in Young Indian Lawyers Association and Others (petitioners) Vs State of Kerala and Others (respondents)*, 28 September 2018.

10 Chakraborty, Abhishek, 'Sabarimala Ban a "Form of Untouchability", Says Justice Chandrachud', NDTV, 28 September 2018, https://bit.ly/3Se8DF6, accessed on 19 October 2022.

CHAPTER 5

1 'Turkey's Erdogan Says Hagia Sophia Becomes Mosque after Court Ruling', CNBC, 10 July 2020, https://cnb.cx/3TeDMtD, accessed on 18 October 2022.

2 'Pope "Very Distressed" Over Turkey's Hagia Sophia's Conversion to Mosque', *The New Indian Express*, 12 July 2020, https://bit.ly/3VCovnT, accessed on 19 October 2022.

3 'World Council of Churches "Dismayed" at Hagia Sophia Shift', *The Indian Express*, 12 July 2022, https://bit.ly/3g6vzth, accessed on 16 November 2022.

4 'Erdogan Rejects Global Criticism over Hagia Sophia Decision', Aljazeera, 11 July 2020, https://bit.ly/3gkwZQi, accessed on 19 October 2022.

5 Priolkar, Anant Kakba, *The Goa Inquisition: The Terrible Tribunal for the East*, Rajhauns Vitaran, 2010.

6 Jain, Meenakshi, *Flight of Deities and Rebirth of Temples: Episodes from Indian History*, Aryan Books International, 2019.

7 'Twitter Hides Trump Tweet for Glorifying Violence', BBC, 29 May 2020, https://bbc.in/3EBUHS3, accessed on 16 November.

8 Feiner, Lauren, 'Twitter Flagged another Trump Tweet for Violating Its Policies', CNBC, June 2020, https://cnb.cx/3ESWOBn, accessed on 19 October 2022.

9 Constitution Annotated, https://bit.ly/3SmfEUM, accessed on 19 October 2022.

10 'Citizens United v. Federal Election Commission', *Britannica*, 21 January 2010, https://bit.ly/2FVh7wu, accessed on 19 October 2022.

11 *Supreme Court of the United States Citizens United, Appellant V. Federal Election Commission,* Legal Information Institute, https://bit.ly/3SVXKYV, accessed on 31 October 2022.

12 Silverleib, Alan, 'Gloves Come Off after Obama Rips Supreme Court', CNN, 28 January 2010, https://cnn.it/3ERd6uA, accessed on 19 October 2022.

13 'What USCIRF Is', United States Commission on International Religious Freedom, https://bit.ly/3EUPeX5, accessed on 19 October 2022.

14 De Roover, Jakob, 'USCIRF Hypocrisy: It Is about the Protestant Worldview, Not Freedom of Religion', *Firstpost*, 11 May 2015, https://bit.ly/3yT7AUe, accessed on 19 October 2022.

15 'Universal Declaration of Human Rights', United Nations, https://bit.ly/3DaGKtk, accessed on 19 October 2022.

16 *Rev Stainislaus Vs State of State of Madhya Pradesh & Others, January 17, 1977,* India Kanoon, https://bit.ly/3TwlfIU, accessed on 19 October 2022.

17 Hughes, Bettany, 'How Christians Destroyed the Ancient World', *The New York Times,* 8 June 2018, https://nyti.ms/2y06OYz, accessed on 19 October 2022.

18 Mugovera, Gracious, 'How Christianity Destroyed Africans', *The Patriot*, 29 November 2019, https://bit.ly/3TN5AWa, accessed on 31 October 2022.

19 Borona, Kendi, 'Why Colonial Christianity Is the Biggest Problem in Africa: An Illustration', *The African Exponent,* 29 January 2018, https://bit.ly/3VHVHdA, accessed on 19 October 2022.

20 Dees, Diane E., 'African Pentecostal Christians Destroying Ancient African Cultures in Nigeria', *Mother Jones,* 6 September 2007, https://bit.ly/3MNsI4o, accessed on 19 October 2022.

21 Griffith, Ralph T.H., (trans.), *The Hymns of the Rigveda,* Second edition, Kotagiri (Nilgiri), 1896, p. 506, https://bit.ly/3DOPXYR, accessed on 1 November 2022.

22 Goel, Sita Ram, *The Calcutta Quran Petition,* Voice of India, New Delhi, https://bit.ly/3Sg2k3S, accessed on 19 October 2022.

23 'United Nations Declaration on the Rights of Indigenous Peoples', adopted by the UN general assembly on 13 September 2007, https://bit.ly/2SfIrLV, accessed on 19 October 2022.

CHAPTER 6

1 Jagannathan, R., 'Shashi Tharoor's "Why I am a Hindu" Is Driven by a Degree of Schizophrenia on Hinduism', *Swarajya*, 20 February 2018, https://bit.ly/3ERl2vXm, accessed on 19 October 2022.

2 'Hindutva Is an Assault on Hinduism: Shashi Tharoor', *The Economic Times,* 29 September 2019, https://bit.ly/3SgzK2C, accessed on 19 October 2022.

3 Aiyar, Swaminathan S. Anklesaria, 'What Hindutva Trolls Can Learn from Gandhi', *The Times of India*, 16 August 2020, https://bit.ly/3DaX5yc, accessed on 19 October 2022.

4 Farley, Harry, 'Who Founded the Church?' *Christian Today,* 14 June 2016, https://bit.ly/3Xkonum, accessed on 19 November 2022.

5 Said, Edward W., *Orientalism*, Vintage Books, 1979.

6 Eck, Diana L., Chapter 1, 'A Sacred Geography, An Imagined Landscape', *India: A Sacred Geography*, Three Rivers Press, New York, 2012,p. 6.

7 Ibid.

8 Jagannathan, R., 'India Is the World's Largest Territory That Is Up for Grabs by Predatory Forces', 10 May 2018, *Swarajya*, https://bit.ly/3Dd1NvB, accessed on 20 October 2022.

9 Sanu, Sankrant, 'Hindutva is Hinduism that Resists', *DNA*, 14 January 2020, https://bit.ly/3eJu7vZ, accessed on 20 October 2022.

10 Harikrishnan, Charmy, 'RSS Is a Lot More Diverse Than It Used to Be: Author Walter Andersen', *The Economic Times*, 4 August 2018, https://bit.ly/3UdZRs7, accessed on 31 October 2022.

11 Jagannathan, R. 'March to Monotheism', *DNA*, 19 November 2013, https://bit.ly/3Vip6dJ, accessed on 16 November 2022.

12 'Full Text of "Moses and Monotheism"', Internet Archive, p. 35, p. 36, https://bit.ly/3FPJ9M7, accessed on 1 November 2022.

CHAPTER 7

1 Talageri, Shrikant G., 'A Short Note on the Varna System and the Puruṣa Sūkta', 23 June 2022, https://bit.ly/3Tiy5ec, accessed on 20 October 2022.

2 Biswas, Premankur, 'Genetic Study Suggests Castes Began to Dictate Marriage from the Gupta Reign', *The Indian Express*, 16 February 2016, https://bit.ly/3eNNAf8, accessed on 20 October 2022.

3 Fárek, Martin, et al., 'Introduction: Caste Studies and the Apocryphal Elephant', *Western Foundations of the Caste System*, Palgrave Macmillan, 2017, p. 4.

4 Jagannathan, R., 'S.N. Balagangadhara Interview Part II: Brahminism and Other 'Isms' Are Inventions of Western Indology', *Swarajya*, 15 April 2022, https://bit.ly/3EWzP8t, accessed on 20 October 2022.

5 It is an approximate number arrived at by adding temples under various Hindu Religious & Charitable Endowments Department (HR&CE) ministries in the South.

6 Banerjie, Indranil, 'Ramakrishna Mission's Non-Hindu Claim Causes Dismay Among Many of Its Followers', *India Today*, 15 February 1986, https://bit.ly/3TEFEvg, accessed on 18 October 2022.

7 Mandal, Dilip, 'Becoming a Hindu Is Not That Easy. Even If a Wasim Rizvi Turns into Jitendra Tyagi', *ThePrint*, 10 December 2021, https://bit.ly/3TwIgeE, accessed on 18 October 2022.

8 Neelakandan, Aravindan, 'Do You Really Need to Specify Your Caste before Ghar Wapsi? And Other Questions, Answered Here', *Swarajya*, 21 December 2021, https://bit.ly/3yWpgOT, accessed on 20 October 2022.

CHAPTER 8

1 Ambedkar, B.R., *The Decline and Fall of Buddhism in India*, Blumoon Books, 2000, Chapter 9.

2 Murphy, Bill, 'China, Officially Atheist, Could Have More Christians Than the US by 2030', *Houston Chronicle*, 22 February 2018, https://bit.ly/2oyHlxE, accessed on 26 October 2022.

3 'Most Christian Countries 2022', World Population Review, https://bit.ly/3VVKaYm, accessed on 26 October 2022.

4 Tabor, Celina, 'About 30% Of American Adults Are Now Religiously Unaffiliated, Pew Research Study Finds', *USA Today*, 14 December 2021, https://bit.ly/3sOPzmZ, accessed on 26 October 2022.

5 Sherwood, Harrriet, 'Vatican Signs Historic Deal with China – but Critics Denounce Sellout', *The Guardian*, September 2018, https://bit.ly/2OMfkOP, accessed on 26 October 2022.

6 *20th Livestock Census*, 2019 report, Ministry of Fisheries, Animal Husbandry and Dairying, https://bit.ly/31xLZxp, accessed on 26 October 2022.

7 'Displaying Holy Cross No Ground to Cancel Scheduled Caste Certificate, Says Madras HC', *The Times of India*, 7 October 2021, https://bit.ly/3N8xOZ9, accessed on 26 October 2022.

8 Varma, Pavan, *Adi Shankaracharya: Hinduism's Greatest Thinker*, Tranquebar, 2018.

9 'Korean Churches Lose Young Congregants, Who View Religion as Irrelevant', *The Ground Truth Project*, 25 April 2018, https://bit.ly/3W5uYIc, accessed on 26 October 2022.

10 Kancharla, Bharat, 'What Is the Change in Hindu & Muslim Population Share Between 2001 & 2011?' *Factly*, 3 September 2019, https://bit.ly/3twHrYo, accessed on 15 November 2022. (The first table in this *Factly* report shows the fall in Hindu and Muslim shares between 2001 and 2011 censuses. Yellow lines show loss of Hindu share, and blue ones gain in Muslim shares. Most states showed loss of Hindu shares.)

CHAPTER 9

1 'Religion Census 2011', https://bit.ly/2IsSLPY, accessed on 15 November 2022.

2 C., Surendranath, 'Why Crypto-Christians May Be Keeping Tamil Nadu's Numbers Below Actual Levels', *Swarajya*, 22 February 2021, https://bit.ly/3O5jktn, accessed on 15 November 2022.

3 Sherwani, Arfa Khanum, 'As Muslims See Sharpest Drop in Fertility Rate, Hindutva Propaganda Falls Flat', *The Wire*, 10 May 2022, https://bit.ly/3gKRO80, accessed on 26 October 2022.

4 Quraishi, S.Y., 'Islam Is the Pioneer of the Concept of Family Planning – And It Is a Myth That Polygamy Is Rampant in India', *The Times of India*, 25 February 2021, https://bit.ly/3SBcigI, accessed on 26 October 2022.

5 Aiyar, Swaminathan A., 'Why Fears over Rising Muslim Population Share, Immigration, Are Unfounded', *The Times of India*, 2 October 2021, https://bit.ly/3TDHjSq, accessed on 26 October 2022.

6 'Total Fertility Rate Down across All Communities', *The Times of India*, 8 May 2022, https://bit.ly/3fatJHi, accessed on 26 October 2022.

7 Aiyar, Swaminathan A., 'Why Fears Over Rising Muslim Population Share, Immigration, Are Unfounded', *The Times of India*, 2 October 2021, https://bit.ly/3TDHjSq, accessed on 26 October 2022.

8 'Covid Forces India's Former Gulf Workers to Forge New Futures', Aljazeera, 31 March 2021, https://bit.ly/3SC1DCn, accessed on 26 October 2022.

9 Connor, Phillip, 'India Is a Top Source and Destination for World's Migrants', Pew Research Center, 3 March 2017.

10 'Census 2011: Assam Records Highest Rise in Muslim Population', *The Times of India*, 22 January 2015, https://bit.ly/3sHkktM,

accessed on 31 October 2022.

11 'The Rise and Rise of Muslims in West Bengal', Centre for Policy Studies, https://bit.ly/3sJpyW2, accessed on 1 November 2022.

12 'Independent Inquiry Must on Alarming Muslims Birth Rate in Kerala: Nambiar', *Business Standard*, 17 September 2017, https://bit.ly/3D9J0QD, accessed on 26 October 2022.

13 C., Surendranath, 'The Real Number of Andhra Pradesh Christians Is Grossly Understated: Here's Why', *Swarajya*, 16 February 2021, https://bit.ly/3zg10aG, accessed on 26 October 2022.

14 'Ruling YSRCP MP Admits Large-Scale Conversions Are Happening in Andhra Via Money Power of Christian Missionaries', *Swarajya*, 26 May 2020, https://bit.ly/3TSt6ka, accessed on 26 October 2022.

15 C., Surendranath, 'The Real Number of Andhra Pradesh Christians Is Grossly Understated: Here's Why', *Swarajya*, 16 February 2021, https://bit.ly/3zg10aG, accessed on 26 October 2022.

CHAPTER 10

1 Jagannathan, R. 'Love Jihad, Conversions: Five Asymmetries That Hindus Must Come to Terms with', *Swarajya*, 25 November 2020, https://bit.ly/3DcnScg, accessed on 26 October 2022.

2 Rehman, Asad, 'Allahabad HC Says Previous Orders on Inter-Faith Marriages Not "Good Law"', *The Indian Express*, 25 November 2020, https://bit.ly/3N7x0Dz, accessed on 26 October 2022.

3 Ambedkar, B.R., Chapter X, 'Social Stagnation', Part IV, 'Pakistan and the Malaise', *Pakistan, or the Partition of India,* https://bit.ly/2osI4nz, accessed on 26 October 2022.

4 Taleb, Nassim Nicholas, *Skin in the Game: Hidden Asymmetries in Daily Life*, Allen Lane, London, 2018, Book 3, Chapter 2, 'The Most Intolerant Wins: The Dominance of the Stubborn Minority', p. 80.

CHAPTER 11

1 'In Muslim-Majority Indonesia, Ex-President's Daughter Converts from Islam to Hinduism', *India Today*, 27 October 2021, https://bit.ly/3N6wlCk, accessed on 26 October 2022.

2 'UP Shia Wakf Board Ex-Chief, Waseem Rizvi, now a Hindu, Takes

Name "Jitendra Narayan Singh Tyagi"', *ThePrint*, 6 December 2021, https://bit.ly/3zeHUC0, accessed on 26 October 2022.

3 Pandey, Ashish, '"Issue Is Disrespect of Islam, Not Him Becoming Hindu": 2 Cong Leaders Call for Murder of Waseem Rizvi', *India Today*, 9 December 2021, https://bit.ly/3f7USdP, accessed on 26 October 2022.

4 'Supreme Court Dismisses Waseem Rizvi's PIL Seeking to Delete 24 Verses of Quran', *The Times of India*, 12 April 2021, https://bit.ly/3f5bAdV, accessed on 26 October 2022.

5 'Hindu Leader Kamlesh Tiwari Killed over Remark against Prophet, 5 Arrested: Police', *Outlook India*, 19 October 2019, https://bit.ly/3N9uflk, accessed on 26 October 2022.

6 'Noting Death Threat to Nupur Sharma, Supreme Court Offers Her Relief', NDTV, 10 August 2022, https://bit.ly/3zqCdkk, accessed on 31 October 2022.

CHAPTER 12

1 Kalning, Kristin, 'Christian Yoga: Trading "Om" for "Amen"', *Today*, 21 May 2012, https://on.today.com/3DBnXI9, accessed on 26 October 2022.

2 'India festival at Yamuna to Go Ahead amid Green Concerns', BBC, 9 March 2016, https://bbc.in/3SC2hjm, accessed on 26 October 2022.

3 'Has Isha Encroached upon Forest Lands? Hear the Truth about This...' Isha, https://bit.ly/3FmLOfM, accessed on 26 October 2022.

4 Haazek, Khan, 'Amarnath Yatra and Its Devastating Effect on Fragile Ecology. Is This Yatra Really an Ecological Terrorism in the Name of Faith?' *Medium*, 2 October 2021, https://bit.ly/3svlkB5, accessed on 26 October 2022.

5 Webster, George, 'Holy Cities Face Threat from Polluting Pilgrims', CNN, 9 November 2011, https://cnn.it/3zk5ltv, accessed on 26 October 2022.

6 Malhotra, Rajiv, 'Why the Kumbh Is at Risk', *Swarajya*, 25 November 2015, https://bit.ly/3DVF5IR, accessed on 31 October 2022.

7 Vadiyala, Ranjith, 'Atrocity Literature: A Western Recipe to

Dismantle India and Hinduism', *Indiafacts*, 25 October 2016, https://bit.ly/3D9xtki, accessed on 26 October 2022.

CHAPTER 13

1 Roy Chowdhury, Debashish, '*The Kashmir Files*: How a New Bollywood Film Marks India's Further Descent into Bigotry', *Time*, 30 March 2022, https://bit.ly/3THXXjY, accessed on 26 October 2022.

2 Kak, Sanjay, 'The Dangerous Truth of *The Kashmir Files*', Aljazeera., 13 April 2022.

3 Mogul, Rhea, 'India's Latest Box Office Smash, "The Kashmir Files", Exposes Deepening Religious Divides', CNN, 28 April 2022, https://cnn.it/3TVsMRR, accessed on 26 October 2022.

4 Mustafa, Faizan, 'Can Hindus Be Minority?' *The Tribune*, 25 September 2019, https://bit.ly/3TV2KOw, accessed on 26 October 2022.

5 @ThomasSowell, Twitter, 4 May 2018, 3.28 a.m., https://bit.ly/3DQNQ5y, accessed on 26 October 2022.

6 Pawariya, Arihant, 'One Blooper on Evolution, & Satya Pal Singh's Crusade to End Minorityism and Free Temples Is All but Forgotten', *Swarajya*, 22 January 2018, https://bit.ly/3gJJGoe, accessed on 26 October 2022.

7 Jagannathan, R., 'SC's Padmanabha Swamy Verdict Is a Cruel Joke, Rich Temple May Be Reduced to Begging Bowl Status', *Swarajya*, 14 July 2020, https://bit.ly/3f2AHOB, accessed on 26 October 2022.

8 'Sree Padmanabha Swamy Temple Faces Financial Crunch amid Lockdown', *Matrubhhoomi.com*, 5 June 2020, https://bit.ly/3Dcx4gW, accessed on 27 October 2022.

9 Full Text of Sree Padmanabha Swamy Temple Judgment of Supreme Court, dated 13 July 2020, https://bit.ly/3VZc8Cy, accessed on 26 October 2022, p. 213.

10 Ibid. 215.

11 'Displaying Holy Cross No Ground to Cancel Scheduled Caste Certificate, Says Madras HC', *The Times of India*, 7 October 2021, https://bit.ly/3N8xOZ9, accessed on 26 October 2022.

12 Kumar, Suresh, 'Only Hindus Can Be Hired for Colleges Run

by HR&CE Department, TN Government Tells Madras HC', *The Times of India*, 23 October 2021, https://bit.ly/3TYUVY1, accessed on 26 October 2022.

13 Varma, Pavan K., Chapter 1, 'Hindu Civilisation, Myth or Reality', *The Great Hindu Civilisation: Achievement, Neglect, Bias and the Way Forward*, Westland Books, 2021, p. 27.

CHAPTER 14

1 'Supreme Court judgment delivered on 9 November 2019 in Ram Janmabhoomi case, paragraphs 796–98, p. 921, https://bit.ly/3fbLnKw, accessed on 26 October 2022.

2 Ibid. Paragraph 800, p. 922.

3 Supreme Court judgment in *Dr M. Ismail Faruqui, etc Vs Union of India and others*, 24 October 1994, Para 85, https://bit.ly/2CPhvxK, accessed on 26 October 2022.

4 'What Is the 1994 Ismail Faruqui Judgment?' *The Indian Express*, 27 September 2018, https://bit.ly/3sAqSug, accessed on 26 October 2022.

5 *Citizens United vs Federal Election Commission*, adjudicated by US Supreme Court, 21 January 2010, https://bit.ly/3Fi8Q7C, accessed on 26 October 2022.

6 Doctor, Vikram, 'Hoping for Divine Justice: When Gods Become Litigants', *The Economic Times*, 11 August 2018, https://bit.ly/3DfU7aw, accessed on 26 October 2022.

7 *Indian Young Lawyers Association & Others vs State of Kerala and Others*, Supreme Court judgment dated 28 September 2018, para 105, p. 318, https://bit.ly/2JofIBr, accessed on 26 October 2022.

8 'The Lord as a Juristic Person: What Legal Rights Do Deities Enjoy?' *The Indian Express*, 4 October 2019, https://bit.ly/2AIPNRg, accessed on 27 October 2022.

9 *Shiromani Gurudwara Prabandhak ... vs Shri Som Nath Dass & Ors on 29 March, 2000*, https://bit.ly/3sI7Thl, accessed on 31 October 2022.

10 Jain, Meenakshi, *Flight of Deities and Rebirth of Temples: Episodes from Indian History*, Aryan Books International, Delhi, 2019.

CHAPTER 15

1 The Places of Worship (Special Provisions) Act, 1991, https://bit.ly/3DavMmB, accessed on 26 October 2022.

2 *Dr Subramanian Swamy & Others vs State of Tamil Nadu*, Supreme Court judgment dated 6 January 2014, para 65.

3 Jagannathan, R., 'Hits and Misses of "Free Hindu Temples" Movement after Padmanabha Swamy Verdict', *Swarajya*, 17 July 2020, https://bit.ly/3W4qP7s, accessed on 27 October 2022.

4 *Uthradam Thirunal Marthanda ... vs Union of India on 31 January, 2011,* https://bit.ly/3gQLr2R, accessed on 31 October 2022.

5 Jagannathan, R., 'Hits and Misses of "Free Hindu Temples" Movement after Padmanabha Swamy Verdict', *Swarajya*, 17 July 2020, https://bit.ly/3W4qP7s, accessed on 27 October 2022.

CHAPTER 16

1 *The Commissioner, Hindu Religious Endowments, Madras, vs Sri Lakshmindra Thirtha Swamiar of Sri Shirur Mutt*, Supreme Court judgment delivered on 16 April 1954, https://bit.ly/3syoGmO, accessed on 27 October 2022.

2 Sen, Ronojoy, 'The Indian Supreme Court and the Quest for a "Rational" Hinduism', *South Asian History & Culture*, vol. 1, no. 1, 2009.

3 'Criminal, Anti-Terror Laws Should Not Be Misused to Quell Dissent: Justice Chandrachud', *Tribune India*, 13 July 2021, https://bit.ly/3zj7OnS, accessed on 26 October 2022.

4 'Minorities Must Have First Claim on Resources: PM', *The Economic Times*, 9 December 2006, https://bit.ly/2MIkkE8, accessed on 27 October 2022.

5 Jagannathan, R., 'A Future CJI's Empty Rhetoric, Woke Liberalism, and Why We Should Worry', *Swarajya*, 14 July 2021, https://bit.ly/3U38Oo8, accessed on 27 October 2022.

6 Ibid.

7 Shourie, Arun, *Eminent Historians: Their Technology, Their Line, Their Fraud,* HarperCollins, Gurgaon, 2014.

8 Antony. K.S., 'Left Historians Prevented Resolution of Babri Masjid Dispute, Says KK Mohammed, Former ASI Regional Head',

Firstpost, 21 January 2016, https://bit.ly/3FnjdHh, accessed on 27 October 2022.

9 Kumar Bagchi, Amiya, et al., 'Statement on Ayodhya Verdict', *Economic & Political Weekly*, 9 October 2010.

10 Jain, Meenakshi, Chapter 1, 'Introduction: The Case for Ayodhya', *Rama and Ayodhya*, Aryan Books International, 2013, p. 11.

11 Paul, Cithara, 'Sachar Figures Reveal Bengal Apathy', *The Telegraph*, 9 February 2010, https://bit.ly/3gP7dUQ, accessed on 27 October 2022.

CHAPTER 17

1 Ambedkar, B.R., Chapter XII, 'National Frustration', *Pakistan, or the Partition of India*, https://bit.ly/2P7dA3X, accessed on 31 October 2022.

2 Ibid.

3 Warner, Bill, 'An Ethical Basis for War against Political Islam', https://bit.ly/3f7Jyi0, accessed on 28 October 2022.

4 Das, Madhuparna, 'RSS' Ram Madhav Says Muslims "Need to Give up 3 Concepts": Kafir, Ummah, Jihad to Kill', *ThePrint*, 8 June 2022, https://bit.ly/3SHAIF5, accessed on 28 October 2022.

5 Savarkar, V.D., *Hindu Rashtra Darshan*, Prabhat Prakashan, 2020, p. 34.

6 Mahurkar, Uday, and Chirayu Pandit, *Veer Savarkar: The Man Who Could Have Prevented Partition*, Rupa Publications, New Delhi, 2021, p. 90.

7 Suroor, Hasan, 'RIP Secularism: Let's Try a Hindu Democratic India (T&C Apply)', *The Times of India*, 29 May 2022, https://bit.ly/3U5mBdQ, accessed on 28 October 2022.

8 Blair, Leonardo, 'Nearly 70 Percent of Born-Again Christians Say Other Religions Can Lead to Heaven; Study', *Christian Post*, 21 October 2021, https://bit.ly/3SK10GI, accessed on 28 October 2022.

9 Gecewicz, Claire, 'New Age Beliefs Common among Both Religious and Non-Religious Americans', Pew Research Center, 1 October 2018, https://pewrsr.ch/3U2Sq79, accessed on 28 October 2022.

10 Masci, David, and Conrad Hackett, 'Meditation Is Common Across Many Religious Groups in the US', Pew Research Center, 2 January 2018, https://pewrsr.ch/3W74PJ8, accessed on 28 October 2022.

11 Balagangadhara, S.N., and Sarika Rao, Chapter 8, 'Colonial Consciousness and Secularised Christianity', *What Does It Mean to Be 'Indian'?* Notion Press, 2021, p. 89.

INDEX